SEX AND OTHER SHINY OBJECTS

LAUREN BLAKELY

ALSO BY LAUREN BLAKELY

Big Rock Series

Big Rock

Mister O

Well Hung

Full Package

Joy Ride

Hard Wood

The Gift Series

The Engagement Gift

The Virgin Gift

The Decadent Gift

The Heartbreakers Series

Once Upon a Real Good Time

Once Upon a Sure Thing

Once Upon a Wild Fling

Boyfriend Material

Asking For a Friend

Sex and Other Shiny Objects

One Night Stand-In

Lucky In Love Series

Best Laid Plans

The Feel Good Factor

Nobody Does It Better

Unzipped

Always Satisfied Series

Satisfaction Guaranteed

Instant Gratification

Overnight Service

Never Have I Ever

Special Delivery

The Sexy Suit Series

Lucky Suit

Birthday Suit

From Paris With Love

Wanderlust

Part-Time Lover

One Love Series

The Sexy One

The Only One

The Hot One

The Knocked Up Plan

Come As You Are

Sports Romance

Most Valuable Playboy

Most Likely to Score

Standalones

Stud Finder

The V Card

The Real Deal

Unbreak My Heart

The Break-Up Album

21 Stolen Kisses

Out of Bounds

The Dating Proposal

The Caught Up in Love Series

Caught Up In Us

Pretending He's Mine

Playing With Her Heart

Stars In Their Eyes Duet

My Charming Rival

My Sexy Rival

The No Regrets Series

The Thrill of It

The Start of Us

Every Second With You

The Seductive Nights Series

First Night (Julia and Clay, prequel novella)

Night After Night (Julia and Clay, book one)

After This Night (Julia and Clay, book two)

One More Night (Julia and Clay, book three)

A Wildly Seductive Night (Julia and Clay novella, book 3.5)

The Joy Delivered Duet

Nights With Him (A standalone novel about Michelle and Jack)

Forbidden Nights (A standalone novel about Nate and Casey)

The Sinful Nights Series

Sweet Sinful Nights

Sinful Desire

Sinful Longing

Sinful Love

The Fighting Fire Series

Burn For Me (Smith and Jamie)

Melt for Him (Megan and Becker)

Consumed By You (Travis and Cara)

The Jewel Series

A two-book sexy contemporary romance series

The Sapphire Affair

The Sapphire Heist

ABOUT

The second the test-the-sexy-scenes offer landed in my lap, I said yes.

After all, I've been damn curious about a few things I've read in romance novels. Do buttons truly go flying across the floor when you rip off a guy's shirt? Is staircase sex hella hot or does it leave you with a big old bruise mark on your back? And don't even get me started on all that panty shredding, and whether it even works.

Time to find out as I embark on Project Sexy Scenes Research, at the request of my hotshot book editor bestie.

All I need is a willing scene partner. Enter Tristan, my best guy friend. The witty, tell-it-like-it-is, bearded hottie volunteers for the experiment.

He's also the guy who gave me the most devastating, toe-curling kiss of my life ten years ago. But nothing has happened since then.

And nothing will come between my panties and our friendship now since we have a plan to keep it PG.

But once the buttons start flying, all bets are off...

SEX AND OTHER SHINY OBJECTS

By Lauren Blakely

Want to be the first to learn of sales, new releases, preorders and special freebies? Sign up for my VIP mailing list here!

1

PEYTON

There's just something about white lace.

Though red lace is delicious too.

And I can't forget about pink lace.

Who am I kidding? From satin to silk to cotton, every shade and every style, it all entices me.

There is nothing quite like lingerie to make a girl feel pretty.

My grandma instilled in me this appreciation for intimates. An elegant aficionado of both class and undies, she took me shopping for my first bra when I was thirteen—a white cotton number with lacy embroidery. Lace and I fell in love at first touch, and I haven't looked back since.

My grandmother also taught me the most important thing to remember when choosing indulgent undergarments: "Whoever said sexy lingerie was more for the man seeing it than the woman wearing it had it all backward."

Or, put another way, if you buy a Kelly-green panty and bra set, it damn well better be because you love St. Patrick's Day.

For you.

As one of my semi-regular customers tries on the matching set, I'm hoping the confident and brainy Daniella is keen on all things Irish for her underthings.

From the privacy of the dressing room suite in the back of my Madison Avenue boutique, she shouts out to me, even though I'm only feet away, sorting through an order of bustiers. "Peyton, I need your prediction. What is the likely outcome of me wearing this set?"

"Let's see what we're working with." I set the gorgeous black satin darlings in their box as Daniella opens the scalloped door a smidge.

A nagging worry pricks at the back of my mind, since she's not a shy woman.

She nudges the door the rest of the way.

"You look like a gorgeous four-leaf clover, and it fits you perfectly." It's true, but something is still off.

She giggles, and my Spidey senses tingle again. Daniella isn't a giggler. She's chatty and analytical, a statistician who loves to talk about outcomes and probabilities, not the type who titters demurely at a compliment.

Hmm.

If this color and this style make her giggle, is it right for her? I don't want her to go home with something that makes her feel anything less than fabulous. Some women love bright green. Others do not. And if Daniella's not enamored, this lush ensemble will wind up in the back of the drawer, aka the lingerie graveyard. It's a fate no sexy underthings should suffer.

And it's not good for the peddlers of them. Let a customer go home with something she won't wear, and you might as well say sayonara to that client.

So, for both our sakes, I pose the key question. "How does it make *you* feel?"

With the door open, she regards herself in the mirror inside her dressing room. "It's an odd color, but Jamie says he loves this shade of green because of . . ."

I wonder what goes in the blank that she hesitates to say.

Money?

Christmas?

Wait. No. I've got it.

"The Green Lantern!"

She swivels around, her jaw falling to the plush rose carpet of my shop. "How did you guess?"

I smile, because now we're getting to the heart of the matter. "I can tell you, but you're going to have to keep it a secret. Pinky swear?"

Her eyes glitter with the promise of intel. "Of course."

I cup my mouth, whispering, "I have lingerie ESP. It skips a generation, but it's passed on through the women in my family."

She laughs, then gestures to her pile of clothes on

the pink cushion in the corner of the dressing room. The top item is a pair of gray panties that look like they've seen five too many years. "As you can probably tell, I don't have any predictive power of the sort. But seriously, did I tell you about his *Green Lantern* obsession last time I was here?"

I shake my head. "No, but you did mention his predilection for comic books the other week. You said he likes it when you dress up as Wonder Woman, right?"

"He's obsessed with her," she says in a whisper, then shudders, like the thought makes her skin crawl. "And that's the heart of the issue right there. He wants to rip my panties off when I wear red and blue. I bought a pair of bright-red satin panties last time, and I wore chunky gold bracelets on my wrists to complete the look. He went crazy for it."

"And do *you* love that?"

She shrugs, a disinterested look in her eyes. "It's not really *my* thing, nor are ripped panties, because . . . hello! All I can see are numbers, numbers, numbers of how much money I'm setting on fire. Can you say 'expensive habit'?" She fiddles with her bra strap. "But aren't relationships about give and take?"

"Of course. But the underwear is on *your* body. Turn around. Look in the mirror. And tell me how *you* feel in this set."

She screws up the corner of her lips and makes a strange clucking sound as she regards her reflection.

One eyebrow lifts. Then the other. She narrows her gaze then gasps, horrified. "I'm the Keebler elf."

I clutch my belly, laughing, till I collect myself. "First of all, you don't look like the Keebler elf. He wears red and yellow with his green jacket, and I would never let you pair those colors."

"You are a good woman to look out for potential color mishaps."

Smiling, I meet her gaze. "However, if you *feel* like the Keebler elf, then the question is—is that what you want? If so, I say to each her own fetish and kink, and nom-nom-nom."

She cringes, shaking her head. "I'm all for kink, but I assure you, a little elfin magic doesn't go a long way for this girl. Or any way, for that matter." She appraises herself once more, studying her reflection. "Nor does leprechaun kink. Admit it: I kind of look like I'm about to skip over the rainbow with a pot of gold."

I laugh, flicking my red hair. "Preach, sister. I can't wear green lingerie for that same reason. And it's a shame, because I love emerald, but I also love sapphire, so I wear that instead."

"For your . . .?"

She waits for me to fill in the dots—*husband, wife, boyfriend, girlfriend, lover.*

I shake my head. "I've been single for some time now, but that doesn't stop my lingerie habit. I wear sexy undies every day because they make me feel fabulous. And I suspect they've played their part in making me feel like I'm finally ready to date again. But listen, I'm willing to bet that your guy doesn't *actually* care what color your panties are."

"You think he'll be fine without the Green Lantern thing?"

I smile softly. "If he loves you for you, and I bet he does, he'll be happy if you're happy. Because pretty panties don't have to be for him. They're about what you like. What type of panties make you want to march up to him and rip off *his* shirt?"

"That's a smart way to look at it. What does get me going?" She repeats the question like she's thinking about it for the first time. "Besides, of course, when he cleans the kitchen and the bathroom."

"That's a turn-on, for sure. Keep thinking along those lines. And when it comes to lingerie, ask what style gives *you* the confidence of Athena? What look makes you imagine you're a Botticelli? For some women, it *is* green lingerie. For others, it's sapphire or ruby. I could bring you a cranberry-red set if you want."

She shakes her head, and I keep going.

"Some prefer sheer nude. Others feel sexiest in a sports bra. Maybe it's a cami and a tank and boy shorts. Or perhaps it's a festive little novelty set."

She points at me excitedly, like she's found the winner in three-card monte. "Yes. *That.*"

I had a feeling I'd pique her interest. She likes unconventional answers, and I bet she'd want unconventional underwear. "Would you say you like numbers?"

"However did you know?" she asks dryly.

"Just a lucky guess," I tease. "Okay, I've been on the hunt for some fun patterns. Let me grab something from a shipment that came in the other day that I think is perfect for you. I suspect you're a big fan of purple."

"Is that your lingerie ESP again?"

My eyes drift down to her handbag. It's a bright shade of eggplant. "Or it could be that your purse was the giveaway."

"Look at you, using observable possibilities."

I curtsy. "But let's make sure you like it first." I step toward the back of the shop, then I stop, going for the pièce de résistance—the proof that I will always put my money where my ESP is. "And if you don't feel gorgeous in this set, your next purchase is on me."

Her eyes pop. "Whoa. Thank you."

I send a silent wish to Grandma Mimi that I'm not wrong here with my lingerie magic eight ball as I fetch the items I have in mind from a box in the back. As I pass, I glance toward the shop floor where my sales assistant, Marley, is gift-wrapping a purchase for a woman in a camel trench coat. *I bet it's red and lacy.*

I return to the dressing room and hand the silky items to Daniella.

A minute later, she gushes her praise from inside the room. "This. Is. So. Me."

Yes. That's what I want to hear—her own confidence in what she wears underneath her clothes.

That's what matters. She doesn't even need my seal of approval as long as she's given it to herself.

She opens the door and strikes a ta-da pose, owning it. The lavender bra and panties decorated with numbers, formulas, and mathematical symbols fit her personality like a glove.

"There is a one-hundred-percent chance of me loving this and feeling hot in it."

"Then I'd say it's a sure thing that you'll be ripping his shirt off when you see him, and he'll love that too."

Her eyes twinkle with naughty mischief. "He will. Because I'm not Wonder Woman." She gestures to her body. "I'm a sexy statistician. Thank you for helping me see that."

"It's my pleasure. I'll be up front when you're ready."

A minute later, she's practically floating as she brings the new ensemble to the register. "Now I only have one thing I want you to remember," I say as I ring her up.

She clasps her hands, waiting for my wisdom. "Tell me."

My expression turns full-on serious. "As much as I want you to come back and buy a new set every single day, remember if Jamie rips this off you, you'll be spending a fortune. Don't do that crazy stuff unless you want to start wiring half your paycheck directly to me."

"I do like your shop," she says with a smile, glancing around You Look Pretty Today, settling on the other patterned bras I recently added. "But I'll take the advice, and I'll tell my friends all about this place. My best friend is a novelist, so I bet she'll dig that type-writer-style over there."

Cha-ching. "She'll look like a decadent wordsmith when I'm through with her."

As I fold tissue paper around the garments, Daniella tilts her head and asks, "What makes you feel like a Botticelli?"

Sliding one finger under the shoulder of my shirt, I show her a hint of the coral-pink lace bra. "Lace. It's my kryptonite, and it's my armor. I've worn lace every single day since my fiancé left me earlier this year. Lace helped me get over him, because every day I had a secret, and the secret was how I looked and felt."

Daniella slowly claps. "When you get back out there, some guy is not going to know what hit him."

I smile as I tuck the tissue paper—covered bra and panties into a bag and hand it to her. "A girl can dream. Thanks, Daniella. Go be the statistical goddess you are."

"That's the only kind I know how to be."

After she leaves, Marley scurries over to the counter, beaming. "You sold the math bra. I thought for sure that was going to wind up in a pile of regrets."

"Regrets are for haircuts and exes. Never under-wear. Not if we can help it."

She offers a hand to high-five. "You're like the lingerie guru. Just like you were in your old blog."

I high-five back as my chest twinges with a smidge of regret. Fine, regrets are *also* for shuttering blogs for the wrong reasons.

But I'm on the other side of those wrong reasons, and the other side of heartbreak, hurt, and doubt.

And there's no time like the present to let the many months of lace work its restorative magic. Perhaps it's finally time to ask out that sweet guy in my favorite yoga class. The one who spreads out a mat for me every time. The guy who also does the best downward-facing dog, and I'm not just saying that because his butt has been carved by angels.

Though those are the best kind of rears to stare at in yoga.

When the bell rings on the pink door, I set aside my yoga-guy musings. A leggy brunette in skinny jeans and a half shirt strides inside, her trimmed abs on display. A honey blonde in a leopard-print skirt is next to her.

My internal radar beeps, and I size them up based on first impressions alone. *What would they like most from my store?* I just stocked the cutest black-and-white animal print that I bet the blonde will go gaga for, and I have new demi-cup bras that I suspect the half-shirter will dig.

"Happy Saturday. If you need any help with styles, sizing, or recommendations, just let me know."

"Thanks, babe," says the half-shirter.

I head to the counter, Marley by my side, and we set to folding the last of the most recent shipment of bustiers we recently added to our wares.

The blonde drags her finger along a shelf, considering the displays. "Oh. This is so fab," she says when she finds the black-and-white bra.

"It's *so* you, sweets. So totally you," her friend echoes. "You have to get it. Seriously, I command you. Now. Get it. Wear it. Be hella hot." She finishes her order with a snap of the fingers.

Marley nudges me, a gleeful grin on her young face.

I simply smile, hopeful for another sale.

"I'm doing it, I'm doing it!" the blonde says, her hand darting into the stack, hunting, I presume, for just her size.

But she freezes.

Flinches.

Gasps.

She calls her friend closer, points excitedly out the window, and whispers. "Babe. Oh my god, look! Do you see what I see?"

The half shirter squeezes her friend's arm. "Your eyes. They're like the best. The best of the best."

"We are so there."

In a split second, the blonde tugs the half-shirter out the door. The two *babes*, as they call each other, race off, the bell tinkling sadly behind them. I have a sinking feeling I know what caught their attention.

My gaze follows them.

The chain store behemoth a city block away sports a new sign in its window: *Half off Lingerie at Harriet's Wardrobe.*

My shoulders slump. "You've got to be kidding me."

All these years of busting my butt to give customers

beautiful underthings and personal service, and here's the specter of the Lingerie Warehouse threatening to devour my little boutique like the blue-plate special.

That's what I'm up against—a wasteland of bargain-basement polyester and panty lines.

2

TRISTAN

It can only be a Monday.

Consider the evidence. An email from a pasta supplier to say he's running late with his gnocchi delivery. *By a week.* A note from my wine guy saying he's out of the chardonnay I ordered. Then a text from my dishwasher calling in sick—for his shift on Thursday.

Not anything I want to see when I check my phone after I get out of the shower. Definitely not all at once.

I need coffee. And I need it stat. After pulling on jeans and a Henley, I brew some French roast and sink into a chair at the kitchen table, fueling up to tackle the rest of today's inevitable flat tires.

"Good morning." My brother, Barrett, strolls out of his room and grabs a box of cereal from the kitchen counter.

"What's so good about it?" I grumble.

He shakes some cereal into a bowl, pours some milk, then joins me, nodding at my coffee mug. "You should stop drinking that. It stunts your growth. We learned that in health class the other week."

"You're seventeen. I'm twenty-nine. I'm fully grown."

"But *what if?* What if new scientific research emerges proving our potential for growth doesn't end when we turn eighteen?"

I give him a stare and my best *I can't even with your sass this morning* face. "That. Won't. Happen."

"It could though. Science expands the boundaries of knowledge every day. Heck, you can clone a dog now. What if we can grow into our thirties?" He shoves a spoonful of cereal into his mouth and crunches hard.

"I'm six feet tall. So are you. We're good to go in the height department."

He shrugs. "If you say so, but I won't stop hunting for new discoveries."

Ah, youth. "My brother, the painter-slash-scientist."

"I'm a Renaissance man. A regular Leonardo." Barrett digs again into his bowl, going from crunching to slurping so loud he might be sucking each Cheerio up with a straw.

I aim a withering glare over the rim of my coffee mug. "I'm pretty sure Leonardo was not a savage at the breakfast table."

He slurps more. "But are you certain?"

"I'm positive. Also, there are these things called manners. You've heard of them?"

The corner of his lip twitches. "Hmm. *Manners.* Sounds vaguely familiar."

"Here's a refresher, then: don't slurp cereal."

He narrows his eyes, making a show of analyzing my wisdom. "But is soup okay? What about ice cream? Is it okay if I slurp ice cream?"

"I see you took an extra dose of sarcasm this morning. Is this because I told you to shut it down and stop watching *Doctor Who* at midnight?"

He scoff-laughs. "*Doctor Who* is so last year. It was *Stranger Things*, and I watched it with Rachel." A small smile flits across his lips but disappears so quickly I could have imagined it.

Except I don't think I did.

And it's more evidence that my brother has it bad for his best friend, and has for some time. But he's afraid to make the first move, so I've been hunting for gentle ways to nudge him.

But I'm not feeling so gentle this morning, so I stay on topic. "Point being, it was a school night, and you still have classes."

He answers my remark with another slurp.

Groaning, I drop my head in my hands. "Dear God, grant me the patience to handle this child raised by wolves."

"Maybe you're the wolf." He laughs, and then the seventeen-year-old little shit proceeds to throw back his head and howl at the top of his lungs. It lasts for a full thirty seconds and incites a frenzy of barking from the terriers who live down the hall.

"You should definitely consider a career in animal

impressions. From the slurping to the howling, you've got a handle on the call of the wild."

His hazel eyes, the same shade as mine, twinkle with mischief. "Know what else I could make a living at?"

"What's that?"

He leans on the elbows he's parked on the table. "Getting your goat. Doesn't matter how much I dangle the bait—you still bite. React like I'm the most teenaged teenager ever put on earth. But no. I'm your wiseass brother, sent here to wind you up forevermore. And doing it most excellently." He lifts his spoon like a hoity-toity society dame and proceeds to finish his cereal ever so elegantly.

Damn. He got me again. I was sure he was a mannerless, cereal-slurping adolescent. I didn't consider he was being uncouth on purpose. And I do ride him hard on civility, since there's no one else around to tell him when he's oinking too much.

"Fine. You win," I concede.

He pumps a fist. "And it's not even seven."

He picks up his bowl and takes it to the sink, and I get a look at what he's wearing.

No effing way.

I hate to go all *kids today*, but I swear. Kids today. They dress like gym class will break out any moment and they have to be prepared. He might have won the slurping showdown, but I draw a hard line at gym shorts on a school day.

He heads to the bathroom down the hall and turns

on the sink tap to brush his teeth. I follow him. "Do you have sports practice today?"

He shoots me a look like I'd said it in Martian. "I don't play sports."

"Oh." I furrow my brow in exaggerated confusion. "Then why are you wearing basketball shorts to school?"

His *duh* look is well-honed from practice. "Everyone wears basketball shorts. And I have a pair of jeans in my locker in case I get busted."

"That's my point. We don't need to tango with the law—not when you go to a freaking magnet school."

"But I look good in these shorts."

I lift a brow. "Are you sure?"

He recoils, jerking his head back. "Are you saying I don't?"

I shrug, scratch my jaw, adopt a casual stance. "I'm saying there are ladies who prefer a sharp-dressed man. One lady in particular."

He spits the rest of the Crest into the basin and snaps his gaze to me with keen but wary curiosity. "What do you mean?"

My brother lights up whenever Rachel is around. Hell, he sparks at the mention of her. But she won't wait for him forever.

I know what happens when you wait too long—the window of opportunity slams shut and you lose your chance. I won't let him make the same mistakes I've made. Not if I can help it.

Ever so casually, I stroll out of the bathroom,

trailing the bait a little. "Just that a certain someone might have remarked she likes a well-dressed man."

"Who?" He's on me like sticky tape.

I stare at the ceiling in the living room, tapping my chin as if thinking hard to recall. "Let me see. I believe it was the sweet and funny girl you had over last Thanksgiving, and Christmas, and so on. She and Peyton were talking about clothes, and she remarked how much she likes a dapper look."

"'Dapper'? She said 'dapper'?"

I nod. "She definitely said 'dapper.'"

He weighs this, then nods. "Sounds like her."

"And it can't hurt to impress the woman. Speaking of, how did it go when you asked her out the other night?" I ask, since he'd hinted that he had something to tell her—that he has feelings for her, I presume.

He huffs. "It takes time. It's like a painting. It's not something that's going to come together all at once."

I grab my coffee cup and take a fortifying drink before I turn more serious. "Look, Barrett. I'm not saying it's going to come together all at once with you and Rachel. And maybe it never will. Maybe her feelings aren't the same as yours. But let's be honest—you've had it bad for her for a while. Do you think you might want to ask your best friend to—oh, I don't know, call me crazy—go out with you before you graduate?"

He sighs, sliding a hand through his floppy brown hair. "Maybe you don't get it. It needs to feel right. When I tell her, it needs to be perfect. Know what I mean?"

The question gives a glimpse of the vulnerable underbelly that he rarely shows. I let down my guard to match.

"Yeah, I do. And I hear ya." Oh, hell, do I hear him. "I've been there. But I don't want you to wait too long and then regret it. You could ask her to the upcoming dance. Worst case is you go as friends, and you're already friends."

He shoots me a look like I just opened his medicine cabinet without permission. "How did you know about the dance?"

I tap my chest. "Guardian here. It's my job to know what's going on."

"You read entirely too many school emails."

"Yes, I do. Such is the fate of a responsible adult. And since I read my emails, I learned of the tragic shortage of chaperones for the homecoming dance and volunteered."

He groans. "You're joking."

"I'll pretend I don't know you. Fair?"

"How does that constitute fair? I think fair would be more along the lines of me having the apartment to myself for a week."

I roll my eyes. "Anyway, wouldn't homecoming be a great opportunity to ask Rachel to go with you? And maybe you'd want to look a little more . . . dapper."

Muttering under his breath, he stomps off to his bedroom. A minute later, he returns wearing jeans and a Henley. Just like me.

Victory is mine.

Standing, I scan his attire with an approving nod. "Well done. You look sharp, my man. Very sharp." I squeeze his shoulder, meeting his gaze. "Now, I know you like this woman. Think about finally asking her out. I don't want you to look back and wish you had."

Slipping away from my grip, he grabs his backpack from the floor, shouldering it. "If I ask her out, you'll stop bugging me about my clothes?"

"News flash: I'm always going to bug you about your clothes."

He smiles then brings me in for a hug. "I know. I appreciate it."

In moments like this, I can handle the insanity of his   now-I-like-you-now-you're-the-worst-person-ever teenage ways. I hug him back and ruffle his hair. He grumbles about it because that's what we do—rib each other and fake-grumble about it—and have ever since he was born, a whopping twelve years after me.

He heads for the door, then turns around, flashes me a grin, and says offhand, "And maybe you should finally ask out Peyton?"

I don't say anything for a minute. Just hearing that name in that context makes my heart beat a little faster than it should.

"Why would you say that?" I ask carefully.

With a gleam of triumph, he points at me. "Why don't *you* just admit you have it bad for her?"

Ah, but there are a million reasons why I don't do that.

Or, really, one.

I tried.

It was too late.

And that was long ago.

That ship sailed, and I had to figure out how to move on. Mostly I do a good job on that front. Or so I thought.

I shake my head. "I don't have it bad for Peyton."

One eyebrow shoots all the way to his hairline. "Really? You sure about that?"

I heave a sigh. "Yes. I'm sure."

"That's not what you said one night many moons ago . . ."

My brow creases. "What are you talking about?"

He taps his temple. "I remember lots of stuff. Including what you told Mom that time."

I wince, a memory taunting me from wherever memories go when you'd like to delete them but can't. "I didn't say anything," I bluff.

"No? You didn't say, 'I've been dying to ask her out since college, and I think I'm finally going to do it'?"

"Doesn't ring a bell," I say stoically, willing my expression to give nothing away.

"Maybe you remember Mom answering." He does a spot-on imitation of our mother. "'Good. You've only wanted to since the night you kissed her during your sophomore year of college.'"

He'd heard that entire conversation? Remembered something I've spent the better part of a decade trying to forget?

Not so much the conversation with Mom, but the

kiss that prompted it. Stuffing it into a mental trunk, locking it, and then throwing away the key.

Barrett opens the door and leaves. But two seconds later, he pops back in. "How about this? If you ask her out, I'll tell Rachel how I feel. Deal?"

I know better than to make deals with the devil, aka little brothers, and say nothing.

He waits, tapping his toe.

I raise an "I've got all day and you don't" brow.

"Think about it," he says, not giving up. "You just said you don't want me to have regrets. Because regrets suck rat tails, right?"

Then he's off, down the hall to the stairwell, and I give the empty doorway the answer to his question about regrets.

"Hell, yes. They abso-fucking-lutely do."

3

PEYTON

Forty-eight hours, and freaking Harriet's is still running its obnoxious sale.

That's why Monday is not the day for me to follow my yoga instructor's advice.

Let go of your worries, Nadia encourages us during our sun salutations in an early evening class after work. I'm sure there's a time for that, but it is not now.

Nor is it the day to finally ask the sweetie-pie guy in class to join me for coffee.

Because, well, he's not here.

And I suppose it's for the best. If I tried to ask him out today, I'd likely botch it. Again. On my first try a few months ago, I was so tongue-tied that he thought I was on Molly.

After class, I sling my yoga mat over my shoulder and say goodbye. "Thanks for a great class, Nadia."

"Thank you for coming. Will I see you tomorrow?"

"That's the plan." I head to change and pop the mat

into my locker before I head uptown in the fading twilight of an early fall night.

My Mary Janes slap the sidewalk of Lexington Avenue, and I stretch my neck, wishing the class had Zen-ified my thoughts. But I'm still thoroughly un-Zen, thanks to Harriet's horrific sale.

There are only two people I can turn to at times like this.

First, Amy.

My friend answers immediately when I call her. "I'm about to run into a meeting," she tells me, "but are we still on for late-night lattes?"

"I'm always up for caffeine. But when did you start having meetings at six thirty at night?"

"I had a brainstorm this afternoon about the next book we're launching, and I want to run my crazy idea past my boss. If she likes it, I'll tell you all about it later."

"I love your brainstorms and your crazy ideas. See you later."

I end the call, turn the corner, and head straight for the other person on my shortlist.

Tristan.

My best guy friend ever.

* * *

I cock back my arm, and with narrowed eyes, I take aim, imagining Harriet's Wardrobe. I picture cloying pink polyester satin, pajama tops dropping silver glitter like dandruff, and cheap ruffled panties that shred on the second wash.

"Porcupine," I curse, grabbing something that Mimi would pull from her handbag of *acceptable* swears.

Then I fling the beanbag at the board.

It misses the hole, skidding past to hit the concrete floor with a splat.

Someone clears their throat, which I can hear because the bar/restaurant is closed on Mondays. A masculine voice rumbles across the game room. "A little less firepower is more sometimes when it comes to cornhole."

"Thanks. Let me see if I can dial myself down."

"It'll be tough," Tristan warns soberly. "Lawn games are played by many but mastered by few."

"Why can't you have ax-throwing here? It would be so cathartic." I can't picture that trendy sport in his eatery, but teasing him is always rewarding. His verbal sparring is on point, one of the many reasons he always resets my mood.

He drags a hand across his scruffy square jaw. "Call me crazy, but I feel like ax throwing mixed with liquor is a recipe for, oh, I dunno, severed limbs and lawsuits?"

"That'd be a no, then?"

His hazel eyes narrow as he puts on a no-nonsense, stern face. "Beanbags are as deadly as you get with me. Take it or leave it." He scoops up a handful, dropping them onto the floor next to me.

Grabbing one, I catapult it and watch as the

beanbag careens past the sweet spot. I stomp. "Who made this game so hard? Axes. I want axes."

He laughs at my plight. "If you're having a hard time with beanbags, what makes you think a deadly blade would be better?"

"Maybe I was a lumberjack in a past life." I finger the hem of my short skirt. "After all, I'm wearing plaid."

With an arched brow, he eyes me up and down, taking in my red V-neck top, my black-and-gray plaid skirt, and my patent leather Mary Janes. I've never met a day of the week that wasn't improved by a skirt.

"A princess lumberjack maybe," he says with a wry grin.

"Great! So you'll have ax throwing installed in time for my birthday, then? Because cornhole is killing me."

He laughs, shaking his head. "Cornhole is easy, Peyton. I swear."

I bat my lashes. "Show me, pretty please."

"You want me to show you how to play the game hipsters can do drunk? You, the badminton champion?"

"Different sport. Also, I've never played before. I'm a cornhole virgin."

"All that time with underthings has really honed your innuendo game." He walks behind me, scoops a beanbag from the pile, and drops it in my palm. I raise my hand to lob it at the sloped board.

"That's your first issue," he says, stopping me before I let loose. "You need to do it underhand."

"Ah!" I knew there must be a trick to it.

"To put it in badminton terms, you're *not* trying to

smack the birdie over the net." He covers my hand with his. "You're gently batting it."

He's closer than I'm used to, and for a flash of a second, it registers that Tristan smells good.

Like pine and soap.

Like the opposite of my ex.

But I push away all those highly distracting thoughts and chant, "Nice and easy." Trying not to inhale another hit of his yummy scent, I gently toss the bag across the board.

It slides into the hole.

"Woo-hoo!" I spin around, thrusting my arms in the air. "Victory! I feel better already." I drop my arms, thinking about the awful last two days. "As soon as that Harriet's sign went up on Saturday, my traffic slowed to a trickle. Today too." A fresh wave of frustration wells up as I picture that stupid banner. "*Half off.* It's a slap in the face to the brand image I've tried to build."

"I know, and we'll figure out a plan. For now, I have something that'll cheer you up more than chucking beanbags."

I rub my palms together. "Is it the owner's special?"

"It is indeed. Close your eyes."

I hum in excitement. This is one of my favorite parts of my visits—when he makes a drink just for me. Each time it's different. Some days call for liquor; others require only soda or tea. Nearly all are delish, and on the mark, because the man has a gift.

I shut my eyes as his hands drop onto my shoulders.

He spins me around, guiding me from the game room to the bar.

"Sit," he says, but I'm not entirely sure where I am. I know the general layout of his restaurant, but I'm blind right now, and don't want to fall on my face.

Story of my life—I don't want to trip, and yet I still do.

Like when I stumbled on my cork-heeled wedges during my eighth-grade graduation.

Or that time I went to my first job interview with my zipper down.

Or, say, the night I tried to treat my fiancé to a sexy surprise.

Even though I'm a lace or bust girl, I donned a satin corset and thong, ready to give Gage what he wanted. He longed for the showgirl look, and I longed to keep him happy, especially since he'd been working so hard, on so many late nights. Time to surprise him with his fantasy, I'd reasoned, and slipped on a trench coat, let myself in at his place, dropped my coat, and struck a pose.

And discovered his executive assistant in a pose too.

Reverse cowgirl, to be precise.

And she looked better in a bustier than I did.

All those late nights working, he'd been cheating on me with her. I bite back the shame that crawls up my throat at the memory.

That was nearly nine months ago. Now I've sold

the ring, licked my wounds, and taken up yoga to make peace with my inner jilted woman.

But all things being equal, I'd rather not land on my ass again.

"What if I fall?" I ask Tristan.

"I've got you." He helps me onto the barstool, his calm voice reassuring. "Just sit."

He moves away, then there's the slide of glass across the wooden counter. My nose twitches happily at the scent of sugar.

"Open your eyes."

I do, and I gasp at the frilly pink drink in front of me, complete with sugar on the rim of the martini glass and raspberries swirling across the top.

"Aww. You made me a girlie drink. And you hate sweets. You must love me, and this drink is proof." Tristan has so much Eeyore in him, and I'm all Tigger. I love poking at that seriousness, and he loves to pretend to be annoyed at my exaggerated shows of affection.

He narrows his eyes and growls. "If you tell a soul I made this drink, I will deny it until the end of my days. And this doesn't change my stance on sweets."

I raise a hand as if swearing an oath. "Harriet's Wardrobe can stick it in their cornhole. And I will keep your secret if your drink is as delicious in my mouth as I suspect it will be."

He shoots me a *did you really just go there* look. "Do you even hear the things you say?"

I blink. "What was inappropriate? The cornhole bit or your drink being delicious?"

"The way-my-drink-tastes-in-your-mouth part." He holds up his thumb and forefinger together, showing a sliver of space. "Just a little naughty."

"Oops. Forgive me." I wink, then take a drink. My taste buds sing a chorus of heavenly aahs, and I shimmy in my seat. "Who knew you could make such a fabulous sugary drink?"

"No one, and that's how it'll stay."

"Wait. All kidding about sweets aside—you're really not going to put this on the menu? This is a perfect cocktail."

He waves like it's no big deal. "Nah, the menu is good as is. The owner's special is just for you."

Just for me.

Those words make my heart glow a little bit.

I down another delicious sip. "Then I am a lucky girl. Because I love the owner's specials. Each one has been amazing."

He raises a skeptical brow. "How is that possible? They can't all be amazing."

"Don't rain on your praise parade. Your drinks make me happy; therefore, they're amazing." I drop my pitch to near his masculine tone. *"Thanks, Peyton. You're the best for saying that. I accept your heartfelt compliments."*

A wry smile tilts his lips as he organizes glasses behind the bar. "Thanks," he says crisply, ready to move on. He's never cared for flowery praise. No surprise—he didn't grow up with *everything you do is awesome* parents like I did.

"You're such an Oscar," I tease.

"And you're such a . . ." He takes his time before he says in an offhand way, *"Pudding."*

I nearly spit out the drink. Speaking of my parents, I scowl at him, wagging my finger. "You're not allowed to call me *Pudding*. Only two people can call me *Pudding*, and neither of them is you."

His brow knits in mock confusion. "No? How about *Dumpling*?"

"You're evil."

"And grouchy? I'm evil and grouchy, right?"

"And you love to make fun of me."

"Can I help it that I have so much to choose from in the childhood nickname department?"

I glare at him. "Just because you know all my family's embarrassing pet names for me doesn't mean you can use them as ammunition."

He shrugs, reaching for a rag and wiping down the counter. "Why do you assume I'm using it against you?"

"Pudding is not a compliment."

His hazel eyes—the color of honey—have a *give Peyton a hard time* twinkle. "Maybe I like pudding. Maybe I like dumplings."

A blush sweeps heat across my cheeks, then down my neck over the rest of me. That's strange. Why would Tristan's remark set off a flash of heat on my skin and a fluttering in my belly? A warm and affectionate glow I understand. A hot wave I don't.

I ignore the tingly sensation and reiterate my point.

"You can't call me *Pudding* or *Dumpling* or any of my dad's other silly little nicknames for me."

"Fine. Fine. I'll behave . . ." He adopts an innocent look, which must pain him, then hits me with *Pie*.

I lunge for him, pretending I'm going to throttle him. "You *especially* can't *ever* call me that." It's the worst of all the hated nicknames.

He darts away but puts on his best contrite face. "Forgive me for calling you *Pie*, Peyton Marie Valencia."

I lean my elbows on the bar and pretend to sulk. "Now you sound like my mother when she's mad at me."

"Yes, but are you distracted from your problems?" he asks with a laugh.

It takes me a moment to realize what he means, and my frown clears. "You did all that to lift my mood?"

"It worked, didn't it? You're not radiating hate fumes like when you stormed in here a half-hour ago. Am I right?"

"Oh, *you*." I tsk, and I smile. "Look at you. Doing that thing where you needle me out of a bad mood."

He blows on his fingers. "When you're good, you're good." He shifts gears to serious though. "But let's tackle the work situation. You're mad at Harriet's Wardrobe for undercutting you. You took it out on the cornhole board, which I approve of as a means of catharsis, even though you're literally the worst corn-holer I've ever seen. Now we need to deal with the reality. Your competition isn't going away, so what are we going to do about Harriet's?"

He puts it so bluntly that my chest pinches, my heart giving an anxious pulse. I've only begun to turn the corner on You Look Pretty Today, and it wasn't easy. I did it with elbow grease, love, and an extra ten grand in new stock—ten grand that came from selling Gage's engagement ring.

Most of the time, I feel like I know what I'm doing when I run the store. But some days, I'm wearing my heart outside my body from the sheer Herculean tasks of the last few years: moving Grandma's lingerie shop from Queens to a new location in Manhattan, slinging it into the twenty-first century, and carrying on her legacy.

Yes, it's a legacy of panties, but it's one the Valencia women love. My grandmother believed in female empowerment before it was cool, and hell if I'm going to break that chain.

Sometimes womanly strength comes from under-things. I want women to feel beautiful, to be their best selves, to ask for what they want in work, in love, in life.

And in bed.

I use underwear to deliver that message to the world.

Lately, though, the task has been tougher, as Harriet's has slowly encroached upon my customer base. But the half-off sign is the last straw.

I could learn from Tristan.

I survey the familiar restaurant, admiring his establishment even after-hours. Tristan has run this place for a number of years, and it's wildly successful. He rolls with the changes too. Operating as a wine and tapas bar at first, he expanded to a full bar recently, and the switch has ramped up sales. Plus, his place is a true neighborhood eatery, enjoying great word-of-mouth and fantastic reviews. He's a whiz at social media, with his fifteen-second time-lapse videos of food prep proving quite a hit on Instagram.

I take another drink and gather my thoughts. "I need to do something to stand out. That's the key." I lower my voice to a confessional tone. "Because these last few months since Harriet's moved in, I feel like Meg Ryan when Fox Books came to town." I frown at the image of the character's shuttered book shop in *You've Got Mail.*

Tristan leans onto his hands on the counter and levels me with a stare. He's not an *everything is going to be okay* kind of guy, so I steel myself.

"This is 2020," he says. "The world isn't so enamored by big box stores anymore. And local business isn't all about discounts. You already have to compete with Amazon and online shopping, so when you're running a brick-and-mortar store, you can't focus on the same things that Harriet's and other big box stores do."

I draw a deep, fueling breath, nodding. "You're right. I need to remember it's about connections. It's about the customers."

"And it's about what you as a business owner can

offer that's special, that the others can't. That's how you need to face the competition."

"I need to do something that stands out. Like what you do with your videos."

He gives me a wry leer. "You could post fifteen seconds of you trying on lingerie."

I grab my napkin, ball it up, and toss it at him. "Smart-ass."

"Kidding, kidding. But seriously, you already have a successful social presence for the store. You're always posting photos of the latest merch, of bras and teddies draped over that chaise lounge." My heart skips down a garden path at finding out he actually pays attention to my social posts. It's kind of endearing to think about him logging into Instagram and scrolling across a photo I snapped of a black lace bra draped on a pink cushion.

"Why not build off that?" he asks. "Or how about doing more on *The Lingerie Devotee*?" He pauses, tilting his head like he's just realized the blog went the way of the dodo. "You only share photos there now. Why did you stop writing posts?"

I sigh with a pang of regret that's chased by a full measure of annoyance. I study my toes while I think, then I meet his eyes, bracing myself to admit a truth I'm not proud of. "Because of Gage."

He frowns like my answer doesn't compute. "Seriously?"

I take another fueling sip of the pink concoction, owning my mistake, even if it made sense to me at the time. "Yes. At first, he thought it was fun. His girlfriend wrote about intimate undergarments, and all that. But when it started to take off, he was worried that my blog was too risqué for his conservative Wall Street world."

My stomach churns with remembered embarrassment. On *The Lingerie Devotee*, I used to weave in tales of how the different items made me feel when I wore them out to dinner or even to the movies. That was too much for him. "Babe, I need you to cool the personal deets for a bit," Gage had said. "When we go to John Fitzgerald's home in Connecticut for dinner or to the Wentworths' fundraising gala, I don't want the partners looking at you and thinking about how you fill out a sheer nightie. That's for me and only me to know. Can we keep it that way?"

Taking a sabbatical felt like one small thing I could do for him. I stopped writing and restricted myself to only posting pics of lingerie.

But since he's no longer in the picture, perhaps I can bring the blog back for me.

"I do miss writing it," I say, running my finger along the rim of the glass.

"Perform a resurrection, then. You don't need to worry about what *he* has to say anymore."

Rekindling the blog sounds like it'd be good for me, and potentially great for business. "True. And this is something I can do that Harriet's can't."

"Let me know if I can help in any way."

"I will. I promise you'll be the first one I call on when the zipper from my bustier gets stuck on a tablecloth as I try on new items."

An eyebrow lifts in question. "How did we get from the bustier to the table?"

I laugh, shrugging. "One of life's many mysteries. Also, you're a genius."

I pop up from the stool, race around the counter, and throw my arms around him. He flinches for the barest of seconds, then wraps his arms around me, inhaling.

Let the record reflect that no one hugs better than this guy. His hugs are warm and comforting, maybe because he's tall and broad, or maybe because he seems to put all of himself into the embrace.

When we separate, I sigh happily. "Have I told you how much I missed this when I was with him?"

"Missed what?" His voice is a little rough.

"You. Me. Hanging out like this. I wasn't able to see you as much as I liked then." I'm acknowledging aloud a truth we're both aware of—we didn't pal around as much when I was engaged.

"He didn't like you hanging with me." It's a statement, not a question, but I answer it anyway.

"He never said as much, but whenever I was going to see you, he'd come up with something for us to do. In some ways, I can understand. It's hard to accept that a man and woman can be such great friends. But you and I are, and I would be devastated if we weren't, Tristan." I haul him in for one more hug.

This man has been in my life since I started college, and we've seen each other through ups and downs over the years—the loss of his father then his mother, the loss of my grandma. We were meant to be friends, and we've only ever been friends.

That is, except for the night before winter break during our sophomore year of college, when he planted the most intense kiss I'd ever had on my lips. A kiss that made my toes curl, made my knees weak. One that haunted my late-night fantasies every single night over the holidays.

But then his father passed away during the break, and when he returned to school, he was understandably devastated. I'd sensed he needed my friendship more than a budding romance, and I offered that—my shoulder, my support. We reverted to the way we'd been before and never spoke of the kiss again.

Now, as we separate, the door swings open. Barrett takes his key from the lock, looks at Tristan, then at me, then back at his brother.

Barrett's grin spreads wider than the Hudson River. "I see you took my advice."

4

TRISTAN

I want to throttle him.

And to think I was simply hoping the little punk would follow his heart's desire and go after the girl.

This is my thanks? No way do I want Peyton knowing she was the subject of a dare to ask her out.

But Peyton can't resist the gumdrop. She perks up, her gaze sliding back and forth between Barrett and me. "Advice? What sort of advice?"

Time to improvise. I can't give my brother a chance to serve up a single tantalizing detail, not about this morning and not about what he overheard years ago. What I'd said then had been true, but I'm not that guy anymore.

I refuse to be the guy pining for someone he can't have. I am most definitely not the type of sad sack who harbors feelings for a woman for a decade.

"He said I should ask you to homecoming," I blurt, falling on the conversational grenade. "That was his advice." Good thing I read those school emails. Good thing I signed up to be a chaperone. "His school has a homecoming dance in a couple of weeks. I offered to chaperone, ergo . . ."

Peyton's eyes glitter with excitement. No surprise. She's outgoing and friendly, vibrant and popular, and has always loved *events*. "Homecoming! Gah! Next thing I know you're going to tell me they're playing badminton there, too, and we all have to wear fancy costumes."

Barrett chuckles. "Sorry, Pey. We won't have your favorite sport at the dance. But it's still going to be hella fun when you come. Isn't it, Tris?" My little brother targets me with a satisfied smirk.

"It's going to be rad," I say, piling it on.

"Absolutely," Peyton chimes in. "And seriously, Barrett—that's so sweet that you told Tristan to invite me."

My brother pastes on a devilishly delightful grin. "I am definitely a sweetheart."

Sweetheart, my ass. "If by sweetheart, you mean he said it'd embarrass him if I went alone, then yes, you can call him a sweetheart for saying I'd bring you to stave off the embarrassment of me."

There. Cover-up achieved.

"Whatever the reason, I'm happy to go." She turns her attention to me, wagging a finger. "And you're in big trouble for failing to mention this sooner. You know I love dances."

It's like she's stabbing me in the heart.

Of course I know she loves dances. The night I kissed her was at a dance party in December. A retro eighties shindig where she rocked out to The Human League and A-ha. Nearly every time a new tune began, she'd shout, "I love this song!" Except every now and then, she'd whisper it. Right in my ear. Making my skin sizzle. Making me nearly lose my mind with longing.

When her favorite Cyndi Lauper song began, her voice turned softer, almost crooning as she'd said, "I always wanted to kiss to 'Time After Time.'"

She'd had a few drinks. Same for me. With liquid courage, I'd said, "So do it."

"Yeah?"

I'd nodded, buoyed by desire and tequila. "Yeah."

She'd inched closer, I'd slid a hand around her waist, and we'd kissed like it was the entire purpose of the dance, of the night, of the entire year.

I'd never wanted to kiss someone so badly. Not before, and not since.

She'd melted against me, sighing and murmuring in my arms.

Now, in the restaurant with Barrett, I shove the memory away, clear my throat, and lean a hip against the bar, presenting my most casual front. "Actually, I forgot how much you like dances. And homecoming nearly slipped my mind, so thanks for reminding me to ask her, Barrett."

"You're so welcome." As he strides to the bar, the look on my brother's face is priceless. It says *You are full of shit, and I love it.*

Meanwhile, Peyton's expression zooms into further delight. "I loved homecoming when I was in high school."

As Barrett plops himself onto a stool, he turns to her. "I bet you were homecoming princess. Did you have a tiara and everything?"

"I was *not* homecoming princess. I was the arty girl playing around with fashion design. I was the girl who made her own dresses. Including my homecoming dress."

"No way," Barrett says, his eyes lighting up.

She straightens her shoulders. "And the yearbook committee named me 'Most Likely to Costume Period Dramas in Hollywood.'" Her expression is pure deadpan. "It was not a compliment."

"What kind of dress did you make for homecoming?" he asks.

She runs her hands over her plaid skirt, as if recalling. "It was a Marie Antoinette style, if you must know."

I stifle a laugh.

"What? I liked frilly things."

"And you still do," I point out.

"It was baroque with poufed sleeves and lace. So much lace. The skirt was so big I could have hidden a small family under it."

Barrett raises a hand. "Peyton, any chance you can still wear that to the dance?"

"Will you be needing to stow away small families under my dress?" she asks.

Barrett laughs, and it's such an honest sound that it surprises me. So much of our conversations straddle the line between brothers who love each other and a parent figure who has to look out for a kid. With Peyton, he lets down his I-love-you-I-hate-you armor. "Sounds awesome," he says.

I point at her. "She's going to wear a costume, and you're worried *I'll* embarrass you?"

He hums, tapping his chin. "Sounds about right. Besides, Peyton's cool. Unlike some people I know." He cough-laughs, then smiles at Peyton, lingering, and a warning light flickers.

Does my little brother have a crush on Peyton?

Is that why he hasn't asked out Rachel? Because he's harboring a crush on an older, unattainable woman?

I groan privately. That would be foolish, but it's entirely possible.

Peyton is . . . well, she's Peyton.

If I were seventeen, she'd be precisely who I'd long for.

She's generous, gorgeous, and one of the kindest people ever.

Her big heart was obvious before, and especially after, we kissed. The next day, school let out for winter break, and I went home to Colorado and helped with my sick dad. I'd planned on asking Peyton out when I returned to school, but the day before I left to go back, my father took his last breath. I didn't go back to school right away, and once I did, I wasn't in a good frame of mind to ask out the most beautiful woman I'd ever met.

Besides, we came from different worlds. She was high class and prep school, with a mother who ran an art gallery and a father who shaped young minds as a professor. My dad had been a construction worker, my mother a bank teller. I was the scholarship kid, and there were plenty of guys in our dorm who had no problem dropping subtle hints that Upper East Side Peyton would only want someone from her fancy neighborhood, not the guy on financial aid who worked in the school cafeteria.

Soon enough, she met Gage from Greenwich, Connecticut, and she dated him that spring. When he graduated, he went to work at a bank in London and told her he'd look her up again when he returned to New York.

A few years later, he did. They rekindled and the rest is history.

Now he's out of the picture again, but it doesn't matter because we're friends—*great friends*—and you don't throw that away on a Hail Mary shot at romance.

Plus, Barrett is my priority. I'm busy finishing the task my parents started—raising him to be a good man.

I return to the topic. "So, the first rule of homecoming is Peyton wears a dress big enough for stowaways and I don't embarrass you. Anything else?"

Barrett drums his fingers on the bar. "That about covers it."

"Count me in. In case I haven't made that clear

already." Peyton pushes back from the stool, grabs her purse, and checks the time on her phone. "I need to go meet Amy and Lola, but the night is young." She flashes me that killer smile then points her fingers at me like a gunslinger—*pow pow pow.* "And thanks to you, I will be blogging tonight. *The Lingerie Devotee* is back."

I mime an epic explosion of awesome with my hands. "*Boom.* The resurrection is upon us."

Barrett even chimes in with an imitation of a heavenly choir of angels. At least, I think that's what his long, sustained *Ahhhhhhh* is supposed to mean.

With a flourish, she waves goodbye, heading out into the New York night. I watch her till the door clangs shut.

"Do you think she knows?" His voice is soft, the question earnest.

"Knows what?"

Barrett's eyes lock with mine. "That it was all a cover-up? That you wanted to ask her on a date for real?"

But that's where he's wrong.

Once upon a time, I did.

Maybe I even planned to try again a few years ago. Perhaps I'd even prepped to walk up to her door with a bouquet of flowers, to swallow down all the nerves in the world, and to ask her to dinner at last. But before I could, Gage returned from London and captured her heart again.

I was oh-for-two, and every baseball fan knows you don't swing on that kind of count.

"That was the past, man," I tell him. "Let it go. I have."

Barrett nods decisively. "That's why you didn't ask her out tonight? Because you let it go?"

"I asked her to the homecoming dance. That's what you wanted, right?"

"No. I thought you were going to ask her for real. I legit thought you had asked her out. That's why I said 'You took my advice' when I saw you hugging her. But instead, you made up the whole lame excuse about asking her to be a co-chaperone. You're always telling me to go for it with Rachel, but then with Peyton, you make it seem like it's this thing you *have* to do, like with homecoming. Why?"

"*Because.*" I draw a deep breath, searching for words. "Because whatever happened in the past, whatever I said to Mom once upon a time, is the past. Peyton and I had a moment, and the moment is over. We are great friends, and she doesn't need to know we were talking about her this morning, okay? That's why I said what I did about homecoming. I don't want her thinking she was the subject of a dare." I drag a hand through my hair, my jaw ticking. "Know what I mean?"

He's quiet for a beat, mulling this over. "Fair enough. I get you." He shoots me a crooked grin. "I mean, I get you by maybe, like, ten percent."

I reach across the bar and tousle his hair. "I'll take ten percent. Anyway, you hungry?"

He pats his stomach. "Always. We were working on sets all night. I'm starving. And since you're the best brother in the world, I was hoping you'd be willing to make me some chicken kebabs."

I smile, because cooking is easy. Whipping up a meal is a walk in the park compared to sorting out the twists and turns my heart undergoes when I think about missed chances with Peyton.

As I cook, he tells me about his day. This is my favorite part of the night—when Barrett relaxes and lets me into his world, a world I never expected to know so intimately.

After we eat, I lock up and we head home.

* * *

Around midnight, I brush my teeth and plug in my phone.

It's dying, down to only 5 percent, but a message blinks at me.

Peyton: Thanks for the nudge! I saw Amy and Lola, and when I returned home I wrote my first post. Here it is.

When I read the blog, I like it more than I should.

5

PEYTON

Amy is buzzing.

She's practically bouncing off the coffee shop walls when I spot her at a table at Doctor Insomnia's after leaving Tristan's.

She launches herself at me as soon as I'm through the door, and our friend Lola, who's joining us, shoots me an apologetic look. "I tried to put a leash on her, but some animals can't be controlled."

"Peyton!" Amy clasps her hands on my shoulders. "I. Have. To. Tell. You. Something."

"You don't say," I say dryly. "Let me guess—you want us to try goat yoga with you? Because you don't need to command an audience with me to get me to say yes to that. I'm there."

Amy's green eyes dance with delight. "Goat yoga! Yes. Sign us up now. Like right now. But this is better."

Lola clears her throat, narrowing her pretty brown

eyes. "But is it better than the Cirque du Soleil class we took a few months ago?"

"Ah, memories." I shudder, as if they were of anything other than the torture Amy exacted on us. I take a seat on the couch, and they follow. "Remember how we all hung upside down in huge swaths of fabric and looked as gorgeous and talented as aerial artists?"

Amy's brow knits with confusion. "Wait. You didn't like the cirque class?"

I shoot her a *you can't be serious* look. "We were terrible. We were like a pack of octopuses on Xanax, climbing curtains."

"But the point was to be terrible. It was cathartic to move like Ursula. We were getting Gage out of your system, and it worked," she says, bopping her shoulders. "He's gone. He's so far out of your system he's practically living on Neptune."

"Amy," I chide. "Don't you know? He resides on Uranus."

She cringes. "Eww. That word is wrong. In my revision of the dictionary, I will abolish Uranus."

Lola cuts in, fanning her forehead. "Please stop saying *Uranus*. It makes me want to pucker my lips, and I suddenly feel moist, so moist all over."

Amy and I crack up, pointing at Lola.

"You win, girl," I say. "Best use of the worst words ever."

Amy mimes removing her tiara. "The crown goes to the esteemed Lola DuMont tonight." She turns to me, handing me a latte she must have ordered for me, then taking a drink of her own. "And I might have another crown for you if you say yes to something."

"Tell me more," I say, rubbing my palms. "What have the two publishing Bobbsey Twins cooked up?"

With her dark hair, carved cheekbones, and chocolate eyes, Lola looks nothing like Amy's cutie-pie next door, but I like to call them twins when they're cooking up schemes. "Are you two starting a new line of lingerie guides and you want me to craft them?" I flutter my fingers against my chest like a delighted starlet, all gracious and surprised. "Because the answer is yes, yes, and more yes."

Amy's eyebrows rise. "Actually, that's not a bad idea." She grabs her phone and dictates a voice memo: "Consider lingerie guides. How the hell is a bra supposed to fit? How do you know what style of undies to buy? And do you have to wash each one by hand and hang them on the balcony to dry?"

"Um, hi. I know the answers to all of those," I say, waving to offer my service.

"I know, but for now . . ." She sets down her phone, takes a breath, and declares, "*Sex and Other Shiny Objects.*"

I look to Lola for an explanation. "I don't have my Amy translator on. Care to tell me what that means?"

Lola flicks her corkscrew curls off her shoulder. "It's a book she's working on. I'll be doing the cover. It's a sexy romantic comedy."

"One of my regular authors is writing it, and I had this crazy idea," Amy adds.

"As you do."

"As I do," she echoes, then pauses for dramatic effect. "To include a companion guide with it. A *Don't Try This at Home* pamphlet, so to speak."

"Don't try romance at home?"

She waves her hand. "No. Of course they should try romance at home. Try it in the office. Try it on the subway. Romance is awesome. But we thought it would be fun to include top tips on how—and how not—to pull off some of the scenes that unfold in romance novels. How to rip off a shirt, how to tear off lingerie, how to disrobe on the staircase without falling on your face. I mean, that is capital *H* hard. How are they all so agile?"

"And you need someone to do what exactly? To write this pamphlet?"

"Yes. Someone daring, willing to try new things. Someone who can make it funny, tell a story. What should you try at home? What shouldn't you try at home?"

Amy's always been wildly inventive, and I'm thrilled she has an outlet for her ideas. Thrilled, too, that she's invited me into her professional world. "Or how about when the hero pulls off the heroine's dress in a split second?" I snap my fingers. "Voilà. One quick move, when I've had to practically can-opener myself out of some of my dresses. How is the hero just whisking it off her?"

"Yes! That's what I want to explore. And all that panty ripping in books. There is so much of it. And in this one—*Sex and Other Shiny Objects*—the hero has a total thing for it. He's obsessed with lingerie, and with taking it off her with his teeth. The heroine calls him the panty shredder."

I clasp my hands to my cheeks, à la Edvard Munch's *The Scream*. "The horror, the horror." I drop my palms. "I was telling a customer this weekend to abstain from that or else she'd be buying out my whole store."

"And that's where you come in," Amy says, her smile brightening.

"You want to buy out my whole store?"

She laughs, shaking her head. "No, but I was thinking perhaps you sometimes have inventory you can't use for whatever reason. Overstock, or maybe damaged goods? Please say yes. It'll help my idea so much!"

"Sure. Of course." Now I see where she's headed with this. "You can definitely use it to test all that panty shredding."

Amy breathes a huge sigh of relief. "Thank you. That helps immensely, because we're on an insane time crunch."

"Problem number one solved. Now we just have to find someone who'll write it," Lola says as she lifts a mug of what looks like chai tea.

"Why doesn't your author write it?" I ask.

"She's busy with the novel itself," Amy says, sighing heavily. "We want someone else to do the companion book. I've scrolled through my list of writers for hire to try to find someone else who has just the right sense of fun and daring."

Someone else.

Those two words hover in the air, swirl around me like smoke wafting through a crisp night. They smell like possibilities. Like turning a corner, like putting yourself out there.

Like standing out.

"You need a writer?" I muse.

"Like a buckle needs a belt," Amy says, sounding urgent.

"Someone to test these ideas?" The wheels are turning, the mental locomotive chugging out of the station and gaining speed.

"Yes. I need to work on finding the right person lickety-split. Because—deadlines!"

"Someone who maybe has done something similar before," I posit, the train speeding headlong down the track.

"Sure. If that's possible," Amy says, tilting her head like a curious pup. "Do you know anyone? I would do it, but my boss wants someone who hasn't read the story yet to test the scenes with fresh eyes and hands."

Maybe it's crazy, but maybe it's not. Perhaps this is exactly what I need to make my blog shine again. To help my store stand out as one of a kind. And, honestly, for me to put myself out there.

Pictures of bras and panties are only so fascinating. The readers seemed to relish the stories behind them, and I did too.

I raise my hand, wiggling my fingers. "I can try it."

Lola nearly drops her cup of chai and blinks at me, her mouth opening soundlessly.

Amy's face has gone stony, my chatty friend uncharacteristically quiet.

I sit back on the couch and savor having rendered two friends, who work in publishing no less, speechless.

A few seconds later, Amy recovers, speaking slowly. "You'd do it?"

"Does that surprise you?"

She nods vigorously. "Yes. A thousand times yes. You stopped doing the blog posts. I know it was because of Gage, but since you haven't picked it up again, I thought you were done with that type of writing?"

"It surprises me too," I say, smiling. "But I'd like to do it."

Her smile stretches around the earth. "It never occurred to me you'd want to. But, oh my stars and garters, you'd be freaking perfect."

"I'm starting to post again tonight. I'm so excited to get back to it." I take a beat. "And I'm going to start dating again. Today I planned to ask out the hot, nice yoga guy. But he wasn't in class."

Amy pumps a fist. "Yes! You've been looking for a new intro with him. This will be perfect."

"'Oh, hey, want to rip lingerie off me? I'll be wearing a tiny thong underneath, though, so no worries —you won't even see my lady parts. 'K? Thanks.'"

Lola's tone goes serious. "Truth though—that's kind of a perfect intro."

"Seriously?" I lift a skeptical brow.

"Why not? It says you're daring. It says you're fun. It's better than 'Want to go out for coffee?'" Lola says in the blandest tone ever.

"It's definitely a conversation starter, and an unconventional date," I say.

Amy's eyes shift from Lola to me. "You'll do it?"

"As long as I can blog about it too."

Amy thrusts her arms up in victory. "It's like you can read my mind. That's perfect. Blog to your heart's content. My boss literally just asked me to find a writer who'd be willing to talk it up in advance, drive interest before the book's release. In fact, the pamphlet can simply be a compilation of your blog posts, with a little tweaking or expanding. You teasing your work with some of these romance novel tropes in real life will actually help build buzz for the upcoming book. Winwin." She takes a breath. "But you're sure you don't mind testing out these scenarios?"

"As long as they don't involve sex," I say, then rattle off a list of sexy times tropes that I could test without getting in the buff.

Amy's grin takes over her face. "This is perfect. Because honestly, we're running behind and we need these, like, end of next week."

I blink, swallowing down the deadline.

"That soon?" I ask, my pitch rising.

"Yeah, we're a little behind. But we just want five common sexy tropes and to demystify them."

That means I'll need to get started tomorrow.

I nod, a dutiful soldier.

"And one more thing," Amy adds.

I brace myself for an even closer deadline.

"Before you do the panty shredding, there's a scenario that's sticking out in my brain that I want you to try first."

She tells me what she wants.

I say yes, praying yoga guy will be downward-facing dog in the morning.

6

PEYTON

The Lingerie Devotee Returns
Blog entry

Hello, my pretties!

I am back!

Did you miss me? I missed you madly.

Exquisitely.

I simply won't let that kind of absence happen again, and that's why, in this installment of *The Lingerie Devotee 2.0*, I give you my solemn oath, sworn on lace, satin, and silk, that I will bring you tantalizing new tales of lingerie, and how it can make you feel.

A picture is worth a thousand words, but words matter too, so I'll be giving you my tales from the lingerie drawer.

For tonight, let me tell you about this lush little number I'm going to wear to bed. It's the kind of outfit that makes you want to turn on Sam Smith, pour yourself a glass of wine, and gaze at the lights of the city.

Solo.

Yes, I have the perfect ensemble if you're enjoying a table for one in bed, because let's be honest, sometimes you only want to bring yourself to the party. You slide into bed, wearing only a pretty little new pair of sleep shorts and a cami tank.

Then you let your fingers do the talking under the covers.

Oh, did I say that?

Yes, I did.

Own it, ladies.

We are owning our bodies and the lovelies we drape ourselves in.

Here's a collection of some of my favorite camis and boy shorts. I chose a pink tropical floral print pattern for its hint of the exotic and paired it with the boy shorts, because it's nice to feel sexy but comfortable too. Here's a pic, all laid out on my bed.

And this is only the start. I have a brand-new series planned for this blog, and it's going to be sexy and funny and clever.

I'm going to test-drive some fabulous scenarios, and I'll report back to you.

Tonight I'll be having sweet dreams indeed.

Stay tuned . . .

Xoxo

The Lingerie Devotee

Find me at You Look Pretty Today on Madison Avenue

7

PEYTON

My tree pose is a thing of legend.

I'm rocking it today, determined to win at yoga, at business, at blogging.

I woke up to five comments, all from prior followers welcoming me back. Go, me.

When the early morning class ends, I roll my mat, turn to the guy who looks like Michael B. Jordan from *Black Panther*, and launch into my best yoga wit. "I'm patting myself on the back today for staying awake during Savasana," I say.

Whoa. That was smooth. Fun and chatty.

"Good for you. Confession: I caught twenty winks during that pose," he says with a smile that lights his face.

"Yoga has many benefits, they say. Catching up on your Z's can be one."

His gaze drifts to the instructor, and he brings his finger to his lips. "Just don't tell Nadia. I'll be in big trouble for snoozing during the most important pose."

"I'll keep your secret."

"Under lock and key, please."

"But of course."

I am buoyed by his replies despite the flock of nervous bird wings that flutter through me. Because the next step is hard.

I've been with one guy for the last few years, and holy hell, trying again is nerve-wracking.

But I remember the yoga instructor's words. *Let go of the worries.*

"So, I have this project," I begin. "It's kind of like a work thing and kind of like a fun thing, but also, like, a cool thing."

His eyes are intense, focused on mine, and I bet this man is a therapist with that whole *I'm listening* vibe going on. "Color me intrigued," he says.

If he's curious, I must be doing this right. "And this is going to sound a little crazy, but I was wondering if you wanted to—"

"Hey, lovey buns."

I jerk my head in the direction of the smooth, sensual voice of . . . my yoga instructor? Why is Nadia talking to me that way? Does she like my butt?

Michael B. Jordan swivels around, meeting her gaze. "One second, sweet ums. I'm just talking to the master practitioner of downward-facing dog."

The instructor beams at us both. "Oh, yes, Peyton is excellent at that pose." She presses her palms together and dips her head. "Namaste." Then to her man she says, "See you soon, and we'll grab some breakfast at the organic cafe?"

He blows her a kiss, and it's like the zipper at the job interview all over again.

He's freaking involved.

And I have egg on my face.

"See you in the next class," she says to me.

His warm eyes return to mine. "Now, you were saying you had a project? How can I help you?"

How about inventing a time machine so we can erase the last two minutes?

I giggle. And, like Daniella, I am not a giggler. But I need to think fast and yank myself up from this pratfall.

"I have this project to . . ." I say, taking my time to regroup and connect some thoughts. What sort of project would I truly talk to him about? I go with the first thing that pops into my mind. "It's a project to encourage couples to shop for lingerie together," I blurt out.

An eyebrow lifts. "Is that so?"

"Yes," I say, taking a breath because I can't get enough air right now. "I have a shop on Madison Avenue. And I would love if you and Namaste came by." *Oops.* That's not her name. "You and Nadia, I mean. I thought you and Nadia might want to come into the shop. And it's half off for you two. Just tell them you know the owner."

His smile ignites. "Wow. Thank you. That is so

kind. We will be there. We are all about exploring sensuality."

"Awesome," I say with a fist pump, praying my face is not the color of a tomato in July.

I give him a business card with the name and location of the shop, then press the gas pedal, hightailing it out of the scene of my latest dignity *kersplat*.

As the morning sun hits my face, I exhale a massive sigh of relief as I rifle through my bag for my phone and turn it on.

I'll just tell Amy I spoke too soon. That I'm not the best woman for the job. That some more adventuresome gal will have to get the job done for her.

She'll understand.

Of course she will.

As soon as the phone boots, I'll send her a note.

But when my phone beeps on, the first thing I see is a text from Amy blinking at me.

Amy: You saved the day! My boss is so excited about the panty shredder!!!

"Porcupine. Cornhole. Fudgsicle," I mutter, then gaze at the sky. "What would you do, Mimi?"

In between the chug of a bus and the squeal of a cab, I listen for her reply. *There is always a plan B. Just make sure your zipper is zipped and your blouse is buttoned.*

As I walk home, I cycle through options.

The delivery guy who drops off packages of silky goodies?

Asking my brother if he or his wife know someone? But they live in Seattle now, so I doubt they've kept up on New York single men.

Do I ask the apps?

Trouble is, I don't know which poison I want to pick.

Before I open the store, I weigh these choices, toying with Tinder and Match and even Boyfriend Material when I'm in the office paying bills.

But I can't quite pull the trigger. Something feels off about asking for help testing romance novel tropes via an app.

These types of scenarios involve trust.

And there's someone I trust completely.

How did I miss the obvious? He's not plan B. He's plan A, and I should have asked him from the beginning.

I open my texts.

Peyton: Remember that time last night when you said you'd help me with my blog?

Tristan: Why do I feel like you're about to cash in on that right now?

Peyton: Because I am.

* * *

My phone buzzes fifteen minutes later.

The text from Tristan says *Knock, knock.*

The store doesn't open for another hour, so I rush from the office, unlock the door, and let him in.

He smells like the fall breeze, and in his jeans and work boots, his pullover shirt hugging his chest, he looks like he's auditioning for a role on *Hardy Men from Alaska.*

He drags a hand through his dark hair. "Let me guess. This is when you tell me you want to do the lingerie videos."

I smack his shoulder, even though he's not far off. "No. But I'll call you when I do."

"I'm going to hold you to that." He surveys the store, his eyes widening as he takes in the sea of pretty goodies. He points to a red bra. "Maybe write about that one next? That gets my vote."

"You love red, don't you?"

"I'm like a bull."

I can't resist. I head to the rack, grab the red bra, and wave it like a matador.

He snorts and kicks his foot.

Laughing, I shake my head. "I swear, you must have driven Samantha insane with your lingerie obsession," I say as I hang the bra back on the rack.

He flinches. "Samantha?"

"Your last girlfriend? Pretty blonde. Ice-blue eyes. Dry sense of humor. Ring a bell? She was the workaholic attorney who drove you crazy because she expected you to be available at midnight to service her."

"Did I say that bothered me?" he asks wryly.

A plume of jealousy rises out of nowhere. What the hell is that about?

I turn around so he can't see my face. But that doesn't change this odd sensation like my shirt is too tight or my skirt is scratchy, when neither is the case at all. But his question leaves me out of sorts. Why the hell am I bothered that Tristan enjoyed sleeping with his ex-girlfriend? I squirm uncomfortably, needing to eject that idea from my brain before it takes hold.

I adjust a pale-pink bra, focusing solely on the here and now, sweeping away images of him with someone else.

"Glad you enjoyed it," I say with the reserve of a hostess at a fine restaurant.

"What I didn't enjoy was her expectation that I pay more attention to her than Barrett," he adds.

I spin away from the rack and look at him again. "Oh. I had no idea that she said that."

"She was oddly jealous of my little brother." He lifts his hands in a shrug.

I rein in the sliver of a grin, even though I'm more

pleased than I have reason to be. "And I guess that's why she's the ex."

"Indeed it is." He parks his hands on his hips. "What's the blog idea? And how can I help? If it involves me lifting heavy boxes, you're going to owe me lunch, woman."

I smile—he's eased my nerves just by being himself. "No boxes. I promise." I grab his wrist and guide him through shelves of camisoles and undies, bustiers and stockings, marching him to the dressing room area, since it's a good place to chat.

"Fashion show?" He stretches out his neck before he parks himself on the pink chair in the corner.

"Not exactly. But . . ." I take a deep breath, hoping this goes better than my attempt this morning. "I'm hoping *we* can test fashion."

One brow climbs in curiosity. "Explain. Because you should know, I'm not wearing any of that stuff."

A laugh bursts from my throat. "I know. Of course. Definitely not. The testing would be on . . ." I flutter my fingers toward myself.

He blinks, like something is stuck in his eye. "You? You want to test lingerie with me?"

"Sort of," I say, my throat dry because this is much harder than I'd thought it would be. Gage's betrayal did a number on me, and my trust in love, romance, and men is at an all-time low.

I repeat my mantras, though, since I'm trying to move into my future, whatever that entails.

Put yourself out there.

Do the hard things.

Go for it.

"Let me start at the beginning," I say.

"That'd be helpful because I'm a little lost."

I park myself on the ottoman, facing him, and I cross my legs. His eyes drift briefly to the black boots that I've paired with a short purple skirt.

"We will be testing various kinds of fashion. And their resilience under certain conditions."

"*We?*"

I adopt my best sales-y smile. "Well, you know how my good friend Tristan said I should blog again?"

"Smart guy. Also, I read the blog last night. It was . . . interesting."

Wait till he finds out what I'm about to hit him with next. *Deep breath.* "And I need to take it a step further," I say, pushing out the next words. "Amy needs someone to test out a few tropes from romance novels to go along with a book she's publishing, and I volunteered as tribute."

The look on his face is inscrutable. "What sort of things?" Each word comes out like it occupies its own latitude and longitude.

"I'm starting with lingerie stuff, and I was going to ask this guy at yoga class—"

"A guy at yoga class?" His tone could slice a statue.

"There's this nice guy at yoga. He always puts out a mat for me. And you know how Amy and Lola have been telling me to put myself back out there and try again?"

Tristan nods crisply, his jaw set.

"I decided to try, and I started to ask him out, thinking maybe it would be just what I needed. Oops. Turns out he's involved with the instructor, and I need someone I can practice ripping a shirt off of who'll also rip off my panties."

And that came out like a five-car pileup.

Tristan doesn't break eye contact. He gazes at me, unflinching.

His hazel eyes are darker than I've seen them in a decade. They remind me of that one night. The night I can still recall with perfect clarity.

It was only a kiss. It lasted a mere twenty, maybe thirty seconds.

But every second is indelibly etched in my memory.

A shiver runs down my spine as I remember how he wrapped his hand around my waist. How he dipped his mouth to mine. How I felt his kiss radiate in my bones that whole night, and for weeks to come.

But if something more were going to happen, it would have happened already.

He scrubs a hand over his stubbled jaw, his words a command. "Don't ask anyone else."

"Why?" I ask, my voice breathier than I'd expected.

"Because I'll do it."

8

TRISTAN

This fashion show raises an interesting question.

As I leave her store to head to my restaurant, I wonder, *Where does a guy buy a shirt he doesn't give a shit about ripping?*

Clothes are not my forte. Most of mine come from a one-minute search on Amazon, where I buy ten of the thing I like and wear them to tatters.

That makes this shirt quest a quandary.

But it's a quandary I'm glad to have because I don't want any other guy picking out a shirt for Peyton to rip off.

That's why I said I'd handle shirt procurement. Why I volunteered to go to her place tonight. Why I said yes to her request.

No, this isn't my big chance to win her heart. That's in the past.

But this project matters to her—for her store, for her blog, and for her reinvention.

And there's no way I want her to find some other guy to test-drive scenarios with. What if she found someone who didn't respect her? Who tried to take advantage of her?

I shudder at the thought as I return to work, heading for my small office in the back to review orders. Before I start, I send a quick message to my buddy Linc. He's a savvy cat, so I bet he'll know where to find the ideal item.

Tristan: Where do I get a shirt that I can use for ripping off?

Linc: Why, I thought you'd never ask.

Tristan: Yeah, same here.

Linc: Also, I'm going to assume you have a good reason why you want one, and assume I don't need or want to know. I would suggest a trip to Duane Reade. In fact, I'm on my way there right now.

Tristan: Duane Reade sells shirts?

Linc: Duane Reade sells everything.

Tristan: Including button-down shirts?

Linc: Yes. Have you ever tried going to a store rather than Amazoning everything?

Tristan: No.

Linc: Fine. I'll help you. Meet me there.

Fifteen minutes later, I find him waiting for me inside.

"Cue the music for the romantic-comedy shopping montage where the cool guy helps the dorky dude buy a shirt."

I scoff. "I'm the dorky dude?"

He gestures to his charcoal slacks and pressed button-down, in contrast to my jeans and pullover. Fine, he cleans up well.

"Obviously, I'm the cool one," he says. "Ergo, you're the dorky fellow."

"Just help me with the shirts. Also, how the hell did you know they sold button-downs here?" I ask.

He raises a finger, his tell that he's prepping to tell a story. "My sister challenged Amy and me to what she likes to call her Presto-Chango game for a Friday Night Game Night and we had to find and buy items with the clock ticking," he says, rounding the corner of the aisle as I keep pace. "We had to report back with completely changed looks in fifteen minutes."

"Um. Like a new costume?"

"Yes, but I didn't know how we could do it. I was freaking out, to put it mildly.'" He stops in front of a rack of socks like he's a game show host. "It was like a whole new world. The drugstore had undershirts. It sold scarves. Socks. Hats. Sweatpants. And, wait for it, dress shirts. Who knew the drugstore had literally everything?"

"Wow. This really changes my life too," I deadpan.

"And since I became a New Yorker, I like to think of Duane Reade as Crisis Solver Central. After all, we won the challenge and now I know where everything is." He guides me a few more feet to a pack of three dress shirts.

I read the label. "They look like they're made of tissue."

"You wanted something shitty," he points out. "This is for Halloween, I presume? You're doing costume planning, right?"

I shake my head. "Nope."

He narrows his eyes, studying me over the top of his glasses. He snaps his fingers. "Ah. They're for Barrett. Something for the theater tech he's doing?"

Another shake. "Not that either."

"Okay, I know I said I didn't want to know. But that was a lie. I love weird shit. You have to tell me now."

Briefly I weigh telling the truth versus evasion.

But since Peyton's blog is public, and since Linc is involved with Amy, I decide to own up to it. "Amy asked Peyton to test some things for her because of her new book and—"

I don't even have to finish. "Yes, of course. That tracks. That's exactly what Amy would do." Linc hands me a pack of shirts, smacking me on the chest with it. "So, you're the guinea pig?"

"One certified lab rat right here, ready and waiting for Peyton's instructions."

He doesn't say anything for a few seconds, then simply claps me on the shoulder. "Good luck with that."

"What do you mean?"

He levels me with a knowing stare. "I mean, good luck with that."

I don't press. I don't need to. Because I don't need luck. This project isn't about luck.

It's about friendship. That's all.

* * *

But just so I'm fully prepared, and just in case she's keen to know the difficulty involved in ripping off a fancy shirt versus a cheap one, I google where to buy expensive dress shirts, then stop at Barneys on the way home and pick up a few more.

Good thing my restaurant is in the black, because now it's not only funding my brother's school, but also this insane project where the girl I was once crazy for wants to tear clothes off me.

And have me tear clothes off her.

All in the name of research.

Later that night, I shower, trim my beard, pull on

jeans and a T-shirt, and text Barrett that I'll be home late and that I've left some chicken parmigiana in the fridge for him, along with a green salad.

His response?

Barrett: Can I slurp the chicken?

Tristan: If you can, more power to you. Also, you're welcome.

Barrett: Thank you. I'll record a video of my success with the chicken consumption.

Tristan: I can't wait.

I leave, stop in a specialty store along the way to pick up a gift for her, then I head to Peyton's with the gift and the shirts in hand.

It's good that I have extras. After all, if she likes tearing the shirt off me once, maybe she'll want to do it a few more times.

Can't hurt to run through the scenarios more than once.

9

PEYTON

To wine or not to wine—that is the question.

But the answer is obviously wine.

After all, what's the point of alcohol if not to smooth over the awkward moments between friends researching the practicality of different scenes from romance novels, right?

Right.

Or maybe the answer is . . . tequila.

As I stare at the shelves in the liquor store near my brownstone, I consider all the liquid options to take the edge off tonight. Lord knows I'll need a little something to smooth over the jitters.

I'm a jack-in-the-box and have been with each tick of the second hand. Since Tristan agreed to be my test partner this morning, my heart's been hammering at triple-espresso speed.

Fine, I'm *only* ripping off his shirt. But my hands will be on him. I'll be undressing my best guy friend.

A friend I kissed ten years ago.

The thought of removing his shirt makes me . . .

I pause before the tequila, asking myself how it makes me feel.

Nervous? Excited? Scared out of my mind?

I haven't undressed a man since Gage. He's the only one I've been with for the last few years.

Just focus on the mission, not your mind-set.

That's what I tell myself. Besides, liftoff begins in less than two hours, and I need to prep. No time to noodle on squishy feelings that have come out of nowhere.

The question of the hour—tequila or gin. Gin or tequila?

Maybe it's a martini kind of night. Except my talents don't lie in making drinks, shaken or stirred, for super spies, so I bypass that old James Bond standard.

While I *could* ask Tristan to make a special beverage, a good hostess would have a cocktail ready. That's what my mother taught me growing up—*never ask your guests to bring a thing but their presence.*

Tristan insisted on buying the shirts, but everything else will be on my dime.

It should be a simple task to select the ideal drink for our research.

As I wander down the next aisle, I mentally mark the whiskeys and bourbons in the no column. I don't have a fire extinguisher big enough to put out the flames in my throat from those liquors.

When I reach the rum options, I can hear the tinkle

of kettle drums in my head, and I smell the sea breeze as I imagine strawberry daiquiris and piña coladas.

Hmm. Do I want an island drink, a city drink, or a classic drink? Why can't I decide?

I scan the aisles up and down, but I don't know what liquor sends the right message. What exactly does one imbibe to get in the mood to reenact scenes from a sexy rom-com with her best friend?

That persistent flock of nerve-birds descends on me once again, flapping annoyingly, winding me up.

This won't do.

I need to calm down.

I need to relax.

What I truly need, though, is help, so I call for reinforcements, FaceTiming Lola.

"Hey, coolest chick I know," I say when her face appears on the screen.

She flashes me a flattery-will-get-you-everywhere grin. *"C'est moi.* What can I do for you?"

I spin around, showing her the shelves behind me. "I'm faced with a bewilderment of choices. I don't know if I want door number one, two, three, four, five, six, seven, or five hundred."

"I assume this is your lubricant for tonight?"

My jaw falls open, and I whisper out of the corner of my mouth. "We don't need lube. We're not doing that. Also, hello? I'd like to think I don't require lube. When it's DTF time, I'm GTG."

With the most epic of eye rolls, she laughs. "It was a metaphor—the social lubricant of liquor. But

I'm glad you're all ready when it's down-to-fuck time."

"Ohhhhh." Well, fine. That makes more sense. I wave a hand like I can erase my last comment. "Pretend I didn't say that."

"Oh no, I can't pretend, because there's a lesson here. Don't dismiss a little assistance, sweetie. Even if you're good to go, you should try it sometime. It can make sex even better. Sex with yourself, sex with a partner, sex in general. Just because Gage wasn't into experimentation doesn't mean you can't try new things."

I bring the phone to my ear, lowering my volume. "Okay, how did we get from liquor advice to sex advice?"

"Sometimes they're one and the same."

"Also, I'm not having sex with Tristan," I say, quiet but firm. I need to quash that notion. "We're friends, and this is a research project."

"It was a tip for the future. Or, really, for now, since you have the chance to try all sorts of things that your ex wasn't into."

True, Gage wasn't the most sexually adventurous guy. He was a typical horny, three-position, twenty-something guy in the city. That worked well enough for me at the time, and our sex life was . . . standard. But since he'd been two-timing me for months, perhaps he was more experimental than I'd thought. But that also means the sex I did have with him was sex without real intimacy.

Sex without a true connection.

I'm not looking for a sex dungeon or a kink parlor. But at some point, I wouldn't mind knowing what it's like to sleep with someone I can trust.

Someone who isn't looking the other way.

Someone who wants to be with only me.

That's what I truly missed out on with Gage.

"I don't think the issue was that Gage wasn't into trying new things," I say to Lola as frankly as I can, since the memory still hurts at times. "He wasn't into trying new things *with me*."

Lola pounces on my reply. "Don't go there. Gage lost out on you. Don't ever forget that."

"I'll try not to." When I linger too long on the man I thought I'd marry, the wounds can be tender, the betrayal appearing as a fresh bruise. "But it's hard, Lo. I put so much of myself into that relationship. I felt so sure about us for so long. He was smart and clever and doting. Until he wasn't, and I didn't see that coming." My voice wobbles, threatening to break in front of the row of Bacardi.

"Sweetie," Lola says softly, "you weren't supposed to see it coming. He's a cheater, and he pulled off a double act for a long time. You loved him, because you're a true and honest person. But he wasn't a good guy. And even though it hurt like hell, you regained something beautiful when he showed his true colors— yourself, your independence, and your romantic future. The world is your oyster. The bedroom is your oyster."

A smile claims my lips, unbidden and unavoidable,

as I wander toward the vodka. "Okay, how did we get from my liquor choices to my vulnerable underbelly to my oyster of a bedroom?"

Switching back to FaceTime mode, I catch her smiling serenely. "It's just something I've been wanting to tell you for a long time, and the moment seemed right. Don't dwell on him. Keep moving on. You're doing great."

My heart glows a bit from the love of a good friend. "Thank you. Maybe I needed to hear that right now."

"And you need to have some fun tonight." She peers closer to the screen and points behind me. "Pick that."

I spin around. "The Ketel One?"

"Yes. Make a Moscow Mule. Get some copper mugs, some limes, and start ripping that lumberjack's shirt off."

I laugh. Tristan definitely has the whole tall, strong, and bearded look working for him. "Okay. But why a Moscow Mule?"

She stares sharply at me. "Did you want a dissertation or a decision, Miss I-Can't-Pick?"

I draw a deep breath, grinning. "A decision."

She smiles, as satisfied as a cat taking a bath. "Good. Also, the heroine makes a Moscow Mule before the hero comes over, so it'll help you get in character. Maybe read the scene before you rip off his shirt."

"I already have, but don't you worry. I have a plan for making storytime a part of my night."

I say goodbye and snag the Ketel One along with

some ginger beer, lime juice, and a couple of limes, then head to the snack aisle.

There.

I pick up a bag of popcorn. This is just like the time this summer when Amy's brother gave me his extra Yankees tickets and I brought Tristan with me. He adores the boys of summer, and I made a big event of it, picking up pumpkin seeds and peanuts, and we snacked to our heart's content as we rooted for the home team.

Nothing like snacks to recalibrate a girl's pulse.

And to thank a guy for doing her a favor.

I check out, and as I sling the bag over my shoulder, I text Lola, feeling proud of my accomplishment.

Peyton: I have the lube!

Lola: Great. Then why don't you try out chapter twenty-two, page two hundred?

With cheetah speed, I click open the working doc Amy sent me, scrolling to that page in the manuscript. Last night, I read the scene Amy wants me to reenact, but I didn't reach page two hundred. I'm betting Lola is sending me down the rabbit hole of some wildly intense sex scene involving toys or places where the sun doesn't shine.

Instead, I laugh as I enjoy a scene involving door hinges and a handy hero. *Literally.*

Peyton: Hot damn. He fixed her squeaky door like nobody's business.

Lola: WD-40 for the win.

Lola: Also, Moscow Mules are fun . . . and you should have some fun during your research. Now, stop talking to me and get ready.

That's good advice, so I follow it once I'm home.

Even though my clothes aren't coming off tonight, I shower, primp, and snap a photo of a new lavender lace bra and panty set, with an embroidered butterfly between the breasts and at the top of the undies.

Then I slide into the soft fabric.

I stop in front of the mirror, checking out my reflection, savoring the way the new lace feels against my skin, how the bra boosts my breasts.

I feel like me, but a better version of me. The me who's turned the corner. The me who no longer hurts because of the past.

I'm a woman starting over.

Maybe not tonight, but that's who I see. A woman who couldn't have embarked on this quest a few months ago, or even a few weeks ago.

But I'm ready now—for my business, for Mimi's legacy, and for me.

I want to be the woman in lavender and lace.

And I can tonight, because I've healed.

Because when I open the door, I'll be opening it to a man I trust. A man who's willing to do me a favor. I let a smile play across my lips, feeling it deep in my soul.

Turning away from the reflection, I slip into a peacock-blue skirt that hits above the knees and pull on a top the shade of eggplant.

I mix the drinks then find an alt-rock station that seems to be on Tristan's wavelength, and when he knocks, I yank the door open without hesitation, and there he is, looking . . . *wow*.

I can say, even without the benefit of the lube known as liquor, the man can wear the hell out of a white button-down and jeans.

Those nerves? They aren't nerves anymore. They're something else—the flutter of something new.

Or maybe something I felt long ago and had to let go.

That kiss. That incomparable, knee-weakening kiss, miles ahead of any other kiss.

I play it back, and I can still feel the shivers that radiated down my spine that night.

Ten years later, and that kiss still does it for me, and I have an answer to my question.

How do I feel about undressing him?

I feel excited.

That's the trouble.

There's no room for that between us.

But for friendship, there is plenty. After all, this guy is coming through for me, and that means the world to this girl.

"Hey, you!" I say with a grin.

He waggles a gift bag. "I got you something."

10

PEYTON

My best friends know I can be bribed with chocolate.

A mere morsel will convince me to accompany you to that awkward work dinner with colleagues.

A square, and I'll help lug your bags of old clothes to the Goodwill blocks away.

A whole bar, and I'll paint your bedroom wall periwinkle. No, you don't need to help. Sit down, relax, and drink your wine.

When Tristan presents me with not one, not two, but three bars from my favorite chocolate shop in the city, I squeal in delight.

And, even better, he doesn't need to bribe me.

"These. Are. The. Best." Glee doesn't begin to describe my mood right now.

"It's just chocolate," he says, amused, as I clutch the bag.

"It's never *just chocolate*," I correct. "It's my

favorite thing in the world. And you also did not have to bring a gift."

He shrugs a little sheepishly. "It's nothing."

That's where he's wrong. I set a hand on his arm, stopping his attempt to dismiss his own kindness. At moments like this, I can see the divide between our upbringings sharply—my family is all warm and fuzzy, giving out gifts and hugs with abandon, and his was sterner, the opposite of effusive. "It's not *nothing*. I love chocolate. I'm in love with chocolate. Chocolate might be my soul mate, so this is not *nothing*. And I love that you did this." I shake the bars of dark chocolate at him till he smiles. And when he does, my heart dances a little jig. "Also, these are Lulu's Chocolates. They're decadent and heavenly and delicious . . . and I can't wait any longer."

I tear open the wrapper and pop a square of Earl Grey chocolate into my mouth. It melts on my tongue, and I roll my eyes like I'm a chef on TV. "This is what dreams are made of." I break off a square and hand it to him. "Try it."

"I was never a chocolate guy."

"I know you're a salty, but I swear, you will not regret this sweet," I say, goading him with a morsel. I want him to experience the goodness of this treat, the richness of the flavors. I want him to feel what I feel, even about chocolate.

"Not my thing," he says.

"Tristan, this chocolate is conversion-level good.

What's the worst that'll happen? You'll hate it and spit it out? Just try it."

He narrows his eyes, huffing. "I'm only doing this so you'll stop asking."

I laugh, loving that he's bending. "I know. Trust me, I know."

He heaves a sigh, like this is too much. He plucks the chocolate from my palm, pops it into his mouth, and chews.

Anxiously I wait. For a few seconds, he says little. But when he murmurs and moans, I nearly bounce. "Good, right?"

"Fine, this is fucking awesome. Can we eat the whole bar now?"

I wag a finger, smiling like I told him so. Because I did. "This is what happens when you've only ever tried Hershey's. You needed the good stuff. And now you've had it."

"Guess I can't go back now," he says with an easy shrug.

"And why would you?" I ask as I usher him into the kitchen, gesturing to the drinks, grateful I made them. Even with the chocolate, my nerves are resurfacing. Because he's here, and this is happening. This strange crossing of lines that's not quite crossing is starting any minute. "Moscow Mule?"

He lifts a brow in question. "You're making drinks now?"

"Hey! I can handle a basic cocktail. Call it the owner's special," I say, gesturing to my apartment.

"I'm sure I'll love it, then," he says, lifting the mug and offering a toast.

"Also, I thought it might help," I admit, before I take a drink.

"Are you nervous?"

I nibble on the corner of my lips, glad to admit the truth. "A little."

He taps his mug to mine. "Don't worry. We've got this, Peyton."

With that, with his strength, his confidence in our friendship, he defuses the tension. I'm so damn grateful, and I can feel my shoulders relax. "We do, right?"

"Absolutely. May the buttons fly."

"Let the floor be covered in them." I clink back and take a drink.

Tristan does too, nodding in approval at the beverage. "You done good, Cookie."

My brow quirks. "Cookie?"

"I figured it was the only nickname I hadn't heard your parents give you, so I thought I'd give it a shot."

"I like cookies," I say, smiling as I take another drink.

"Also, isn't that what all those romance novel heroes do? Don't they have pet names for heroines? Sugar Lips and Cute Tush and Bumpkin . . ."

I nearly spit out my drink. "I'm positive they don't call the women they're courting *Bumpkin*." I set down the cup and turn to grab the treats I picked up for him. "And I have something for you too." I show him the salt-and-vinegar popcorn, along with a bottle of his favorite IPA. "See? I know you're still a salty guy."

He whistles appreciatively. "Let's get this shirt ripping going so we can have some popcorn."

"Snacks are the way to your heart," I say as I set the bag back on the counter.

He grabs my arm, dropping his tough-guy armor as his voice goes a little softer, more vulnerable. "Thanks, Peyton. For the popcorn and beer. And for knowing I'm a salty."

It's a small thing, but it feels like a big thing too—this acknowledgment that we know what makes each other tick.

That we intrinsically understand each other.

He holds my gaze a beat longer, his hazel eyes warm and intense. My chest has the audacity to tingle. I lick my lips, trying to keep my tone friendly, playful, as I reply, "Once a salty, always a salty. But I'm glad to see you're liking sweets too."

He swallows, his voice a little rough. "Yes, I am."

And it makes me happy that he does.

He reaches behind me for the copper cup, finishes the contents, then declares, "It's showtime."

I'm so ready it nearly scares me.

11

TRISTAN

She's given me gifts before, so I don't let the popcorn and beer go to my head.

She's a gift giver—always has been. Thanks to Peyton's birthday-buying extravaganzas, I have a panini grill, a coffee maker, and a drone.

For various holidays, she's doled out a range of cards: playing cards, Cards Against Humanity, and a gift card to the new Korean restaurant in the East Village that she gave me after I split up with Samantha several months ago.

Over the years, I've received countless gifts from this woman, so I'm not going to read anything extra into something as simple as popcorn and beer.

Do that, and you open yourself up to a world of hurt. After all, when she gave me cologne for Christmas four years ago, I misread the hell out of that. For months, each time I wore it, I was convinced it was her secret way of telling me to go for it with her.

Because each time I wore it, she said I'd smelled *so good*.

That was when I decided to try again with her. Or really, to try for real. To ask her out on a date, once and for all.

And that was when Gage came back to town and won her heart.

I'm not wearing the cologne tonight. I'm not barking up that tree another time.

I'm here to help—that's all. I bought her chocolate because I'm a good guy. Because that's what my mom would have told me to do—*make sure to let a woman know you appreciate her.*

Fine, it's not like I would have asked Mom, or Dad, for input on Peyton's unusual request. And I don't need advice. But I could sense it took some ovaries for Peyton to ask for help, and I want her to feel comfortable.

Hence, chocolate.

I stride into her living room, where she gestures to the couch. This is her show, and she calls the shots. As I sit next to her, she reaches for her phone. "Ready for storytime?"

"I am."

She clicks open a document and reads in a sultry tone.

"*I was pent-up from the night we'd had. From the way he'd talked to me at the concert. From how he'd looked at me in the cab.*"

She stops, purses her lips, and coos. "Ooh."

My curiosity is piqued. "Go on, Cookie. I want to know what kind of night they had, don't you?"

"Oh yes, I do." She returns to the story, shimmying her shoulders like she's having a good time.

I am too, and that both surprises me and doesn't. My e-reader looks like a high school English teacher's shelf: *A Separate Peace*, *A River Runs Through It*, *The Catcher in the Rye*. That's what I dig, as well as the occasional memoir from chefs like Anthony Bourdain, or food blogs that focus on the food rather than the sprinkling of ridiculous adjectives.

I didn't think I'd enjoy listening to a romance.

But I do.

I like listening to her read to me.

"Weeks of this back-and-forth, this cat and mouse, had me so wound up that I was afraid I'd pounce on him. And when considering pouncing, my rule of thumb was better safe than sorry. Otherwise, you could end up with claw marks."

"Claw marks are bad?" she asks with an arch of a brow.

My eyes drift to her nails—not too short, not too long. My mind drifts to possibilities I shouldn't entertain, but I do anyway. "I'm not opposed to them," I admit.

Maybe it's a confession she likes, because her breath seems to hitch as she returns to her reading.

"He dragged a hand through my hair and kissed me deeply as the elevator rose. 'I'd really like to tear your

clothes off when we get to your apartment,' he murmured.

"'Oh, good. I was hoping you were ready to pounce too.'

"'So damn ready.'

"Seconds later, we stumbled into my place, the door slinking shut behind us."

My mind assembles images of elevators; of hands in red hair; of hot, deep kisses.

And I need to wipe my brain free of these dangerous thoughts, so I hold up a hand, stopping her. "How does a door slink shut? Do doors slink?"

She blinks, surprised. "I don't know. Do they? I guess that does sound weird."

"People slink. And animals. But doors? I think they *snick* or *fall* shut. I don't think they slink shut."

She sits up straighter. "I should tell Amy this sentence might need work. *Slink* is a weird word, right?"

"Yeah. Let her know."

She clicks over to her notes app, jots down a reminder, then returns to the document. But before she begins, she shoots me a glance, her eyelids lowering. "You don't like the story?"

"What? Why would you say that?"

"Because of the *slink* thing."

I don't want to admit I like it a lot. But neither do I want her to worry. I set a hand on her leg. "Just read, Cookie."

"I've always enjoyed reading out loud," she says, her tone less nervous, more playful.

"I grabbed his shirt—"

She stops speaking, reads the next lines quietly, then tosses the phone onto the cushion. With a deep exhale, she points to her door. "Let's just do it. Go stand against the door."

Holy hell, that is hot. And it seems to be what we both need. "What the lady wants . . ."

I oblige, heading to the door.

She dims the lights halfway and walks to me, her heels clicking loudly against the floor, the sound reverberating like a countdown. To what? To button blastoff?

Maybe.

It's just buttons, but still, my muscles tense because when she's inches away, all my fantasies from years ago flash before my eyes.

Her. Me. Tangled up together. *Touching, kissing, fucking, feeling.*

I bat them away. Far away.

This. Is. Research.

She slides her fingers over the top button of my shirt, unhooking it quickly.

Then the next.

My skin sizzles. From *that*. From two buttons. I try to redirect with a question. "I thought you were going to rip—"

Her finger lands on my lips. "Shhh."

I fight off my desire to nibble on that finger. To kiss and suck and bite.

I grit my teeth as her hands return to our main business.

She takes a fistful of each side of my two-cent shirt from the drugstore and goes for it, tugging hard.

Nothing happens.

Not a single thing.

The shirt stays on.

"Okay, let's try again," she says, her eyes intense and serious. She grabs hold of each side of the shirt once more, pulling, yanking, and grunting. "This is actually ridiculously hard."

I raise a finger. "Can I give you a tip?"

"Are you an expert on shirt ripping?"

"No, but logic would suggest you might want a little runway. Maybe build up speed unbuttoning the first two then dive into the rip."

Her mouth forms an O. "Yes! That's brilliant."

She buttons the shirt back up, then shimmies her hips, blows out a long stream of air, and sings softly, "Bow chicka wow wow."

I laugh, once more feeling like we're friends who help each other, even with absurd requests.

She undoes the first one, moves a little faster with the second, then yanks at the shirt.

Ripping one side down the middle.

We burst out laughing.

The buttons are all intact, but the shirt has been torn asunder, hanging open.

"Holy shit, Peyton. You did it." I stare at the carnage of the Duane Reade clothes. She's staring too.

Not at my shirt.

At my chest.

Then at my abs.

She looks at my face, her breath stuttering like she's trying to collect herself. Then her eyes roam down. "You. Work. Out."

Every macho instinct in me tells me to preen, to show off muscles that sweat and time at the gym have carved.

But I resist those urges. "Every now and then."

"Shut up. These are religious abs. These require daily practice."

I laugh at her assessment. "Yes, my abs are quite devoted."

She laughs too, then smacks me with her palm. Almost like she's trying to cop a feel. But her hand darts away so quickly that I decide it's just Peyton's usual fun-and-games routine.

Her eyes twinkle with unbridled enthusiasm. "Want to do it again? Since you brought spare shirts. We should definitely do it for research. We need to test the hypothesis more than once," she says, like she just got off a roller coaster and wants to ride it again.

So do I.

All night long.

"Absolutely." No wonder those heroes in romance novels like this so much. It's just fucking hot when a woman wants to get you naked.

It's hot even if it's for research.

I remove the torn shirt and head to the kitchen, where I left my bag.

She's quiet, and the silence is sexy. It says she's watching me. She's looking at me.

When I turn around, my hunch is confirmed.

Her eyes focus on my chest as I slide my arms into another shirt and button it up. She doesn't take her gaze off me. The entire time, she watches, and it's heady. It makes my pulse roar.

I close the distance between us until we're a foot apart. The air is charged, crackling. I can't stop thinking about what happens next. After the heroine rips off the hero's shirt. After she slides her hands along his abs, up to his pecs, around his neck.

When she presses her sweet, lush body to his.

My brain skyrockets ahead, picturing crushing her lips to mine, sliding my hands under her skirt, walking her to the wall.

Having her and pleasing her.

I force myself to stay rooted to the project. This desire is borne out of the moment. It's a normal reaction to a beautiful woman taking off my clothes. Nothing more.

I'm a researcher—that's all.

The renewed focus helps.

Like a diligent scientist, she runs the experiment again, unbuttoning the first button, then ripping at the rest of the shirt with all her strength.

One button comes loose, but it doesn't fall. It hangs by a thread.

She stomps her foot. "I want the buttons to fly off. That's how it happens in the books, and it seems so sexy."

Ah, hell. I need to find a way to deliver for her. "I have one more shirt to try," I say, but I'm not thinking of the third one in the cheap pack. Time to lean on the pricey shirt. "Want to see how an expensive shirt holds up?"

"I do." Her voice is breathy, eager.

Is this turning her on too? If it is, join the club.

Grabbing the Barneys one from the bag, I slide my arms into the sleeves. She stares at me again, her eyes traveling over my biceps, my chest, my abs.

Like she's seeing me for the first time.

Like she's drinking in the view.

She's mesmerized, and her stare heats my blood, driving me on. I stalk over to her, park my hands on my waist, and wait.

Her lips part, and my memory serves up the delicious reminder of how intoxicating she tastes. How sweet she kisses. How softly she sighs.

I clench my fists, staving off my desire.

She lifts her hands, but she doesn't undo the top two buttons. She *plays* with them. Her fingertips fiddle with the first one, toying with it, and with me. With each stroke of her fingers on the buttons, she's also running her fingers over my body, across inches of my chest.

Even through my shirt, she's turning me on.

Like that's a surprise.

"I like these buttons," she says, as if hypnotized.

"Yeah," I say, since I can't really form any other words, let alone thoughts.

She's transfixed, fondling the fucking buttons, and it's driving me insane with lust. If she keeps this up, I might die from it.

"They're so shiny, and they feel so good," she whispers, like she's in a dream. "Who knew buttons felt like this?"

Her voice is like honey, and I want to taste her lips again. Taste her skin. Kiss her everywhere.

That's the problem.

This experiment needs to end before I hit indecent levels on the arousal meter.

"Take it off," I tell her, because I can't handle this much longer.

Slowly, seductively, she undoes the first button. A flash of heat crosses her blue eyes. Maybe it's *desire.*

Did I imagine it?

Is she feeling it too?

Her hands move quickly but strategically, and she undoes another button, then one more, and when she tugs this time, there's a *plink* on the hardwood.

She flinches in delighted surprise.

Another button.

This one goes *ping* on her floor.

And then the rest are flying across her apartment.

Ping, ping, ping.

She's laughing and grinning and staring at the button carnage. "Holy smokes. It worked. It really worked."

I've never seen her this excited. "Damn, woman. You did it," I say, taking in the trail of shiny objects on the floor of her place.

She gazes at them, then at me. "I guess it was the fancy shirt?"

I cock my head. "Was it?"

"Actually, no." She shakes her head, like she's processing what just went down. "For that last one, I think I felt like the heroine in the novel, and that's what did it."

Oh God.

Oh hell.

Oh, fuck me.

I want to dissect that six ways to Sunday. I want to read all sorts of meanings into her remark.

No, I want to read *one* particular meaning into it. But I have to protect myself. This is merely acting.

None of this is real.

After she snaps a picture of the buttons, I put on my armor, pick up the carnage, and pull on a gray T-shirt. I turn the evening in another direction, because it's the only way I can survive this project.

By *not* reading into it. "Want to have that popcorn?"

"I do," she says with a smile, then she raises the lights and grabs the beer she bought me. We head to the couch and break open the snack bag.

"Ladies first," I say, and as she dips her hand into the bag, it feels like a postcoital cigarette.

I grab a handful of popcorn and chew. "I am indeed a salty forever."

"I know you so well," she says, and that's the real postcoital afterglow. Because the popcorn isn't only popcorn. It's evidence that she knows me.

That she wanted me to have what I like.

That she wanted me to enjoy this night.

As I regard her on the couch, legs tucked under her, munching on snacks, grinning happily, I hate that I'm aware once again of how different she is from every other woman I've ever been attracted to.

How warm and open and honest. How giving and caring and loving.

How wonderfully, fantastically different she is.

But learning that anew is exactly what my heart doesn't need. If I stay here, I'll let the popcorn and beer trick me, like the cologne did years ago.

And popcorn is just a snack. Beer is only a drink.

None of these gifts are signs.

Life doesn't give you signs.

Life gives you potholes, and you have to navigate around them without crashing.

After a thirsty sip of the brew and a few more handfuls of kernels, I scoot away from the pothole of desire. "I have to take off."

Her expression morphs into sadness. "You do?"

"Barrett will be home soon," I say, fashioning a plausible excuse.

She frowns. "Too bad. I was going to see if you wanted to watch *The Walking Dead* or something," she says, making me wish once more that I could convince myself to stay.

"Rain check?" I take the empty bottle to the kitchen, setting it in the recycling bin.

"Of course. Go see Barrett," she says, shooing me to the door.

"Let me know when the next session is."

"How's Thursday?"

Grabbing my phone, I make a show of looking at the calendar, tapping my chin, and furrowing my brow. "Let's see. If I move this meeting with a supplier, then if I change my Zumba class, and maybe I can skip flower arranging—"

She clears her throat dramatically.

"Ah yes. I can fit you in at seven fifteen on Thursday. Seems I have an opening then," I say, hoping a little humor will sweep away the lust cloud chasing me.

"Thanks for finding a window," she says, laughing. "Now leave before I kick you out."

"You'd never kick me out."

"I know," she says softly, so softly.

And I know it's true. I grab the bag of clothes, and I go.

* * *

Barrett's not home when I return. He's still at play practice, and he won't be back for another hour.

I knew that.

This little white lie is for the best.

Trouble is, I can't wait for Thursday. Especially when she texts me and tells me how much she's looking forward to the test she wants to run that night.

So am I.

God help me, so am I.

12

PEYTON

The Lingerie Devotee: Do Try This at Home
Blog entry

Lavender is for possibilities.

It's what you wear when you're an explorer, traveling across new boundaries, entering a new land.

Lavender's not brash. It's subtle, encouraging you to try new things.

And try I did.

Last night, I conducted a tasty new experiment.

After all, who hasn't wondered if life could play out like the pages of a romance novel?

The ones where the good stuff goes down.

Where shirts come off and buttons fly.

And I am here to tell you, they can indeed soar.

Powered by lace and lavender, I put on my best bold self, walked across the living room, and tore at a handsome man's shirt.

Okay, moment of truth.

The first time, nothing happened.

The second instance? I ripped the cheap shirt down the middle, leaving two sad shards.

But the third time?

Oh yes, it was a charm.

The buttons flew.

One, two, three, and more.

All of them landing on the hardwood floor.

And the trick I learned is *wanting it.*

Do you want to tear his (or her) clothes off? Then *mean* it. Believe it. Go for it. But do set the stage. Put on some music. Have a drink. Get in the mood.

Wear something that brings you pleasure.

Let yourself feel like the heroine in your own story.

Own it.

And then . . . *do it.*

Whether the buttons fly or fall or stay in place, what matters is what *you* want.

Last night, I wanted to tear this guy's shirt off like I've never wanted to disrobe a man before.

It worked so well, and here's the evidence. A photo I shot of the buttons on the floor. And here's what I wore—my ensemble for my shirt-shredding mission.

When he was gone, I luxuriated in this sexy set a little bit longer, and in the prospect of the nights ahead of me.

Xoxo

The Lingerie Devotee

Find me at You Look Pretty Today on Madison Avenue

13

TRISTAN

Barrett: Dude. She called you "handsome."

Tristan: What are you talking about?

Barrett: Don't act like you don't read her blog.

Tristan: And you do read her blog???

Barrett: Duh. Obviously. Rachel and I are reading it now. We're laughing our asses off. Can you wear that ripped shirt to homecoming? *Handsome.* :)

Tristan: Shouldn't you be in school?

Barrett: It's lunchtime . . . *Handsome.* :)

Tristan: Go eat lunch, then.

Barrett: Go man up. *Handsome.*

Tristan: Goodbye, Barrett. Good luck on your history test.

Barrett: How did you know I have a history test?

Tristan: It's my job to know what's going on with you. Now finish your sushi, drink your LaCroix, and get your butt to fifth-period history to take your test on United States foreign policy in the Middle East.

Barrett: You're obviously a spy if you know I'm drinking LaCroix and eating sushi.

Tristan: Either that or I actually pay attention to your likes and dislikes.

Barrett: I'm going with spy. *Handsome.* :)

14

PEYTON

"That'll be two hundred twenty-one dollars," I say to the petite blonde with a soft Southern accent, who's gobbling up three camis, two baby-doll nighties, and a black slip.

She plunks down her credit card, then flashes a pink lip-glossed grin. "And I'll report back tomorrow. Because I have plans for these darlings tonight."

Arching a tell-me-more brow, I wrap the purchases in tissue paper as Marley scans her card. "Plans with lingerie are the best kind," I say.

Leaning in closer, she offers a whispered confession. "Tonight, I'm thinking of wearing the baby doll, making margaritas, playing D'Angelo, and ripping off my man's clothes."

"And I suspect your report card will include a big S for tonight—S for satisfied." I slide the shopping bag to her, and she takes it, swinging it back and forth.

"I can't wait. Loved your post. Thanks for the tips,

and thanks for the suggestions on these sexy little numbers." She tips her forehead to the bag of items I helped her select. "Now, I'm off to pick up a few shirts for tearing off."

All I can say to that is: "You go, girl."

After she leaves, Marley grabs my arm, clutching my wrist. "She's the second person today to say something about your blog."

"And it's barely past noon," I add, a frisson of excitement darting through me.

But I'm not going to get ahead of myself. Yes, the blog generated more comments today. Yes, two customers have mentioned it. But one resurrected blog is not enough to combat a big box store with a discount sale. I eye the banner in Harriet's window across the block.

"See? Harriet can't mess with us. We always take care of our ladies," Marley says, full of fire and pep, and I love it.

"Exactly. We have a ways to go, but we'll keep it up." I'm a glass-half-full person, though, so I'm choosing to be happy that a handful of customers are devouring my posts and buying some goodies.

Including, evidently, my yoga teacher's beau. Because he strolls in next.

"Namaste," I say playfully, hoping humor will defuse any remaining bits of awkward from the other day.

"Namaste to you too," he says with a grin. Then taps his chest. "Michael."

"Peyton. Glad you could make it in," I say and maybe the awkwardness was only on me. Yes, it was definitely on me.

"I read your blog this morning with Nadia. We are officially lingerie devotees now. Well, she wears the lingerie. I just admire the view."

"That definitely makes you both devotees," I say, and for a fleeting second I'm reminded that I was going to ask this guy whose name I didn't even know till a moment ago to be my scene partner. I'm so glad he turned out to be involved. "Are you looking for anything in particular for Nadia?"

"Something indulgent. She loves satin and lace and I love to spoil her."

"That's our favorite kind of men," Marley chimes in.

"Trouble is—I don't have a clue what to get her. No idea where to start."

"Then you are doubly our favorite kind of guy," she adds.

"Marley, can you help him choose a few potential items?" I ask.

"Would love to. We have some fantastic new items in both satin and lace."

"Take me to them," he says, eagerly.

When they're done, he brings a huge haul of goodies to the register. Whoa. I'm definitely glad he's a customer.

"Glad you found some lovely items. And half off like I promised," I chime in.

He shakes his head. "You support my love's business at her yoga studio. I will support you. No discounts. Just good, honest patronage. It's that simple."

"I'm touched," I say, my heart warming. Maybe Tristan was right—the personal connection is what matters.

And I'm a little richer too when he leaves, a couple bags of goodies in tow.

It's a reminder that I'm on the right path with the blog project.

I need to walk that path tomorrow night too, but the experiment I have in mind requires a different setting than my place.

"Can you man the front for me for a few? I need to make a call?"

"I can *woman* the front," she says with a saucy wink.

"Good catch. My bad. Work your magic."

She makes abra cadabra hands as I head to my Lilliputian office in the back to make the requisite arrangements with my mother for session number two.

She answers on the first ring, and her warm, confident voice is always good to hear. "Hello, sweetheart. What are you up to?"

"Oh, you know. Just causing trouble."

She laughs. "As if. You were never my troublemaker."

"Nor was Jay. Admit it. You raised two good kids despite your best efforts." "True, I did try to corrupt you. But you were so stubborn, insisting on actually listening to me and whatnot." She heaves an exaggerated sigh, and I laugh, enjoying that I don't need to brace myself to make my out-of-left-field request. She's the model of a supportive mom, even when I ask for the unusual.

"Speaking of corruption, I need to borrow your apartment tomorrow. Please tell me you and Dad still have your Thursday-night Scrabble contest at the Bridgertons'?"

"You act like we're so predictable."

"And the verdict is?"

She huffs indignantly. "Fine, we're set in our ways. But why do you need our place?" I hear her snapping her fingers. "Oh! Is it for your blog? I read your newest post this morning. All I can say is *ooh la la*."

I cringe, the fire flaming my cheeks. I'd nearly forgotten my mother was a devotee of *The Lingerie Devotee*. While my love of undies isn't a secret, my blog veered in a much more personal direction last night—one that's not exactly fodder for the family.

Yet I need to own it. This project involves putting myself out there, so I square my shoulders. "Yes, I'm conducting a research experiment," I say, then I dive into the rest of the details—how I'm helping Amy, and that the unnamed man is my best guy friend.

There's a pause, the silence unnerving, till my mom fills it, her pitch rising. "The guy in the blog, the handsome guy—that's *Tristan*?"

She says his name like she's never heard of him,

even though she knows him well. She's met him many times.

"Yes, Tristan."

"He said yes to being your partner in crime?"

"Well, obviously. You read my post."

"Interesting." She says it the way a detective on a TV show would comment on a twist in a case. As if the word can be rolled out on a red carpet.

"Why is it interesting?"

"It's interesting that he's the one you enlisted."

Her logic is a bit circular, so I press further. "Who else was I supposed to ask? He's a friend. A good, trust-worthy friend."

"True. Then be sure to have fun tomorrow with . . . *your friend*," she says, a wink in her voice.

A wink that winds me up. "What's that supposed to mean, Mom?"

She chuckles like I'm oh so silly. "Sweetheart. I've seen how you and Tristan are together. You're great friends, but you also have this . . . what's the word . . .?"

"Yes, what *is* the word?" I'm desperate to know.

She takes another beat, then answers crisply, "Call it a vibe."

A familiar doorbell rings in her home. "I have to take off. There's a package I need to pick up down-stairs. You know the code to get in. And feel free to have dinner when you're done." The sound of the fridge opening reaches my ears. "Let's see. Looks like we have plenty of dishes ready for you. Edamame and roasted mushrooms, veggie lasagna, and some polenta with red peppers. Just don't eat the quinoa. I need it for a cranberry salad I'm making for Friday night."

"I'll do my best to resist the quinoa," I say, making a barfing sound. "I mean, it'll be tough, Mom. But I'll try."

"Quinoa is irresistible, so do try to show some self-control," she says, not taking the bait. "Hands on the man, hands off the quinoa. Gotta go."

She hangs up.

That's how the call ends? With advice to keep my paws off her quinoa?

Staring at the screen, I shake my head, trying to shake off her comments, but one word in particular echoes.

And it's not *quinoa*.

It's *vibe*.

What sort of *vibe* do Tristan and I have? I wasn't even aware we had one.

I tap out a note to Amy.

Peyton: Do I have a vibe with Tristan?

My finger hovers over the send button. But I don't hit it. Instead, I delete the text, letter by letter.

I don't know that I'm ready to hear someone else's opinion when I haven't formed my own yet, so I ask myself that question the rest of the afternoon as I take care of customers, into Thursday, and then later that night as I select my underthings.

Do we give off a sense of *something*? An energy?

I reflect back on the way it felt to tear off his clothes, to discover his strength, to find that flash of heat in his eyes.

Goosebumps rise on my arms, and my breath catches, giving me my answer.

As I slide into a lace plunge teddy, I think my mother might be right.

If there's a vibe, I'm betting it's the boomerang effect of that kiss from ten years ago.

Because Tuesday night, I wanted *that* again.

And I wanted to tear his shirt off for more than knowledge.

For more than the blog.

I didn't simply want to undress him for research. I wanted to undress him for me.

As I find a black dress in my closet, I pause, running my hand over the soft fabric, contemplating, wondering.

What am I supposed to do with this desire?

How am I supposed to manage this new bout of wanting?

I don't know what to make of these feelings. Except this much I know for a fact—it would be a mistake to act on them.

Long ago, we had our chance. Now, we have our friendship, and it's back on solid ground again.

He means too much to me. He matters too much. I won't let anything topple us.

Not even the shiver of desire that shoots down my spine as I head to my parents' Fifth Avenue apartment.

After all, he can't practice whisking off my little black dress while we walk up the staircase at my place.

I don't have a staircase.

My parents do, though, and it's carpeted.

That's great because I suspect I'm going to fall on my ass.

15

PEYTON

The first time we try the scene, my shoe catches the carpet, and I nearly twist my ankle.

The second time, Tristan laughs so hard while trying to tug up my skirt from three steps away that we both fall into a fit of laughter.

The third time most definitely isn't a charm. It's a tumble as he lunges for me and I shriek while we slide down the steps.

On our asses.

But I don't mind falling with him. It doesn't feel like a failure. It feels like a spectacular fail with my best friend. On the bottom step, I collect myself and hold out my hands, flummoxed. "How the hell do they pull it off in the books?"

"Don't you know? In romance novels, everyone is suave and coordinated."

"Are you saying I'm not coordinated?" I ask indignantly as I untangle my legs from his feet.

"You? *No*. Never."

I give him the gentle shove on his shoulder that he deserves. "You're not exactly Fred Astaire."

He grins from his post next to me on the bottom step. "Fine. Let's call a spade a spade. I'm not Fred and you're not Ginger." He smacks his forehead. "Ginger! You are *a* ginger."

I finger a strand of my red hair. "You're just realizing this now? I've known you for ten years. Might want to work on your powers of observation, Fred."

He rolls his eyes. "No, I'm figuring out the perfect nickname for you." He stands, offers me his hand, and pulls me up. "You're Gingersnap."

There's a note of pride in his tone, like he's delighted he devised this term of endearment. And I don't mind Gingersnap. Maybe it's the way he says it—with a touch of affection.

"Fine. I'll be Gingersnap to you. . . *Fred*."

"Then let's do it one more time . . . Gingersnap." His voice is a little rougher, a bit sexier, and it makes my chest tingle.

Exactly what I don't need.

I shake it off, trying to stay loose, to stay in the friend zone.

But maybe I'm too loose, because when he's ready to make the waist-grab move, I wiggle away.

Unintentionally.

Which means my elbow bonks the wall.

"Ouch!" I rub my elbow.

"You okay?" There's genuine concern in his voice.

"I'm not sure I'll live," I say with a pout as the joint smarts.

He reaches for my arm, inspecting it then softly rubbing. "What do you want me to say at your funeral?"

He's deadpan serious, and I nearly crack up. But I rein in my laughter, affecting a high-brow tone. "Please say she died trying to escape a most dangerous staircase undressing. Also, let my death not be in vain." I lift my finger, an orator making a point. "Let it serve as a warning to all those intrepid readers tempted to reenact staircase disrobing."

"You've given your life to a good cause," he says with a solemn nod. "I will carry your warning to the masses."

"You do that."

We make our way back down the stairs, where I try to regroup. We need to fully test this scene before I can report on it in the blog and in Amy's guide. "Okay, let me review the choreography so I know I have it straight," I say, so I don't mess up again. I gesture to the staircase. "I head up the stairs. I glance behind me after three steps. You give me a sexy smolder. I sashay my hips. You reach for my waist, spin me around."

"After that, I lift your skirt," he says. "You take two more steps up. I slide the skirt up your body. Another step. Over your head. You do this all with heels on, and boom. Top step. Birthday suit," he says, dusting one hand against the other.

"I'm not wearing my birthday suit," I point out, but

the thought has me flustered. Or is it flushed? Is that a flush spreading over my chest at the prospect of nudity? But flushes and blushes are precisely what I want to avoid in this scenario. "I'm definitely not wearing it," I say, to drive the point home.

"Actually, you are. We always wear our birthday suits."

I sigh dramatically. "You know what I mean."

"I'm wearing my birthday suit," he says, gesturing to his frame, and for a few deliriously erotic seconds, I imagine him naked.

Strong muscles, carved abs, that sprinkling of chest hair that's the perfect amount of manliness.

My mouth waters.

My stomach flips.

And I reprimand the hell out of my brain, the indecent wench.

Friends don't picture friends in the buff.

"Let's try it one more time," I say with a crisp nod and a cool tone. "We'll do it by the book."

He clears his throat, his tone shifting. "Peyton, I have another idea."

I blink. "You do?"

"I do." He pauses, scrubbing a hand across his chin. "Do you trust me?"

The question is rhetorical. "Of course I do."

He shakes his head, like that's the wrong reply. "I know you trust me. But *can* you trust me right now? To take the lead?" His voice is gentle but somehow commanding at the same time. It's soothing, and the question says he knows me, but he also needs me to let go. To give in to him.

Can I?

Will I stumble if I do?

His eyes lock with mine, and the intensity in his gaze is reassuring, like the security he gave me at his restaurant the other night when he said, *I've got you.*

I give the only answer I can. "I trust you."

"Good. Then let's do it."

"If you say so, Fred."

His lips curve in a crooked grin. "I do say so, Gingersnap."

He hits play on "Wicked Game" on his phone and sets it on the table at the bottom of the stairs, and the smooth, sultry strains of Chris Isaak float through the air.

The music pulses, low and sexy, like it's playing in my body, beating inside me. The effect is heady. It sets the mood for the scene.

A scene we're simply acting.

That's all this is. Acting and reenacting.

He arches a brow, glances at the stairs, then says in a rumbling, sexy voice, "Been thinking about you all day. Need to get you upstairs and get this off you."

He has? Oh, dear God. That's not helping me think friendly thoughts.

Wait.

That's what the hero says in the book.

He memorized it. He learned his lines.

I'm a little relieved he didn't mean it, and a little disappointed too.

But I zoom in on the job. Fortunately, I know my lines too. "Then come and get me," I say, taking that first step in my Louboutins.

The second. And the third.

I glance back. He's right behind me. I wiggle my hips, feeling daring, seductive.

This is when the hero is supposed to tug up the skirt.

But Tristan doesn't lift his hands. Instead, he gestures faintly to the steps ahead of me.

Keep going, they say.

I take another step, unsure of how this scene will play out when he's not quite following the choreography.

"Need you all the way naked," he says, gruff and wildly sexy, reciting the hero's next lines.

"So you can have your way with me," I say, like the heroine does. I take another step, then one more.

He's right behind me, and I don't know what's coming next. He's supposed to yank my skirt up.

But he hasn't touched it.

Instead, I feel a faint brush of strong fingers on my waist.

I shudder. The sensation is almost too much for me to make it to the top of the stairs.

But he nods, urging me on, his hands on me till I hit the landing.

This isn't how the scene unfolds in the book. I

should be naked by now. I'm not even sure what I'm supposed to be doing when he joins me at the top. I feel every sensation in my body, keenly aware of him behind me and of the thread of possibility that winds around me. What will happen next? What will Tristan do?

I look up at him, my breath in my chest, my heart in my throat, his eyes on me.

"It's safer here," he whispers.

And I understand completely what he did.

He abandoned the moves to get me up the stairs safely.

My heart thumps harder.

"And this is where I take your dress off like he does in the book." His words send a shock wave trembling through me.

I know what to do. I know what to say. I don't recite the heroine's lines. I use my own.

"Take it off," I say, feeling daring.

And daring feels spectacular.

Like taking a chance. Like putting myself out there.

His hands dart out to the hem of my little black dress. With a rough swallow, he slides it up. He's not hesitant. He doesn't delay. He lifts it to my waist, only pausing when the bottom of my black teddy appears. His gaze lingers for a moment, then he's back to the job.

The whisking off.

He yanks up the dress to my breasts.

The trembles I felt before? They're nothing

compared to the full-body shudder I experience as I record this moment.

His hands. The set of his jaw. The fullness of his lips.

One more swoosh of fabric and the dress goes over my head. His fingers brush my arms, my shoulders, my hair. The faint little touches set me aflame as he lets the dress fall to the floor.

I'm hotter than a sidewalk in summertime as I stand before him wearing only a lace plunge teddy and black heels.

The question he asked at the bottom of the steps reverberates in my mind.

Do I trust him?

He must know the answer. He must know how much.

Because I'm here, nearly naked, and he made sure I didn't fall.

But sometimes you need to say it twice.

"I trust you." It feels like jumping off a cliff.

"Same," he says, like it's hard to speak even that one word. My gaze slides down his body. His fists are clenched by his sides, and it's as if I've walked in on him in a private act, so I return my focus to his face.

But that feels even more personal because he doesn't stop staring at me, nor do I want him to.

I know that look. It's how I devoured him the other night.

With hungry eyes.

He's drinking me in, eating me up, and I want

everything about this moment to stretch long into the night.

I want to be gazed at this way forever—with adoration, with lust, and with something I've never seen before.

Something I don't know how to name.

The air is thick with desire, wrapped up in the fading notes of one of the sexiest songs I've ever heard and its final warning not to fall.

He breaks the trance. "Nice teddy." His voice is a mere rasp.

"Thanks," I manage to say.

For a long, delirious moment, the hero's next words hover between us.

Now let me see how sexy you look on my bed, wearing nothing but that naughty grin.

I can feel them pulsing in my body.

But he doesn't say them. We've already gone off-script. We're writing new lines, trying new scenes.

And I don't know what happens next.

Tristan scrubs a hand over his stubbled jaw, swallows, and glances away as if it pains him. He bends, grabs the dress, and hands it to me. "Want to go get something to eat? I'm starving."

No, I want to shout. *I don't want to eat. I want to finish the scene. I want you to find me on your bed, wearing nothing but a naughty grin.*

And yet, I can't want that.

My disappointment is chased with relief that he suggested food, an exit.

I need to get out of this zone with him. This lawless land where I'm entertaining wildly dangerous thoughts about my best guy friend.

I have to reset right now. Or else I'll do something we'll regret.

"Yeah, I'm ravenous," I say.

But not for food.

16

TRISTAN

Greasy food.

That's the only solution to tonight's dilemma.

Cheap, grungy, hole-in-the-wall grub.

Something to kill the mood of the black dress, the send-all-the-blood-rushing-south teddy, and that precipice.

That fucking precipice at the top of the steps where all I wanted was to haul her in for a kiss. To slide my hands through that silky curtain of hair. To bring her close and tell her I can't stop thinking about her and *need* to have her.

Instead, I choose a Mexican joint that's as dingy as winter is long. We order tacos, chips, guac, and two Diet Cokes, then snag a Formica booth at the back of the shop, the sharp scent of cleaning supplies from a nearby closet making my nose sting.

I'm not thinking of sex now. I have bleach nose.

Nor am I picturing that teddy I bet she's still

wearing under the hoodie and jeans she changed into. Fine, I am thinking of the teddy, but I'm trying not to.

I divert all my brain cells to the guacamole as I dip a chip then crunch into it.

"What's Barrett up to tonight?" she asks.

"More play rehearsal. The theater department at his school is intense, especially as the show gets closer. He's working on the set designs. He seems to really like it."

She picks up her taco and takes a bite, then says, "I could see him being a set designer someday. Like for Broadway."

I smile as I snag another chip then chase it with a drink of soda. "Definitely. And if not that, he'll be a scientist. He digs science a lot. But hell if I know what it takes to be a scientist. I was terrible at any science classes."

"Same. I wish there had been a way to be a psych major without taking chemistry. But alas, I couldn't escape it."

"You were dead set on studying psych," I say, recalling our college days—business for me, psychology for her. "Did you ever want to be a shrink or a therapist?"

She shakes her head. "No. I just like understanding what makes us tick."

"Ah. Have you figured it out yet, Gingersnap?"

"Still working on it." She digs into her taco, taking another bite and swallowing before she says, "How is he doing though?"

I wipe my mouth with a napkin. "What do you mean? With the set design?"

She shakes her head and sets down her half-eaten taco. "No. Just in general. I know it's been two years since your mom died, but how do you think he's holding up?"

Ah, the million-dollar question. I ask myself that daily, but hardly anyone else does anymore. A few months, maybe half a year, seems to be some kind of statute of limitations on grief, when people stop inquiring.

But Peyton never followed those rules. She didn't follow them in college when my dad passed away, and she didn't follow them, either, when I lost my mom.

Ironic, in a terribly cruel way, that my mom died right when she'd finally started dating again. She'd met a guy she liked. She was moving on from her own grief, moving ahead into the next phase of her life.

But fate has a way of fucking with you, and the bitch had a field day screwing with my mom. One sunny summer afternoon, as she was heading to see her new guy and Barrett and I were at the movies, my mom suffered a heart attack in the park.

She died on the way to the hospital, no one with her but the paramedics.

Watching my fifteen-year-old brother break down, kneeling, bawling, clutching the hospital bed when we arrived damn near broke me too.

I was twenty-seven, and the pain of losing her was excruciating. But I'd lived a quarter-century already. I'd made it through my teenage years with both parents, and through most of my twenties with one.

My kid brother was fifteen and had no one but me. I'd have to be enough.

He moved in with me a few days later, and somehow we've fumbled our way through. I found a therapist for him, and over time, he navigated to the other side of grief.

I take a bite of my taco, putting it down before I answer Peyton's question. "I think he's doing okay. And I mean the good *okay*. Not the *eh* non-committal *okay*."

She smiles softly. "Good *okay* is definitely all right." She takes a sip of her drink and sets it back down. "A lot of that is because of you. You know that, right?"

The praise feels undeserved, and I wave it off. "Nah, he's a good kid. We had good parents. And he had a good shrink."

She reaches for my hand, squeezing it. "Yes, that's true. But mostly what he has is you. You've been there for him. You've helped him."

I shake my head. "I didn't do anything special. I did what anyone would do."

She shoots icy death rays at me with her stare. "Stop. Seriously. Why is it so hard for you to accept a compliment?"

I shrug, sliding my hand away from hers. "Maybe because I don't feel like I did anything. And maybe because that wasn't how I was raised."

She doesn't back down but grabs a chip, scoops some guacamole, and lifts her chin defiantly. "Well, I *was* raised that way. And I believe in draping the people I love in compliments. Heck, I give compliments all day long at my store to strangers. But you?" She points at me with the loaded chip. "I want you to hear this. You need to hear this. You're amazing. And you've given your brother support and security. That you feel it's what you had to do doesn't negate that."

She stabs the air again with the chip, the scoop of green wobbling on the edge. "You're there for him every day. You listen, and you encourage him. You set boundaries and give him what he needs. You're only twenty-nine, and you've had to be a parent—and not at a starter level. You need to accept this compliment. Because you're incredible." She finishes her speech with a final jab of the chip, and the dip splats onto the Formica.

A laugh bursts from my throat.

She stares fiercely at me again. "Don't think the errant guacamole exempts you from taking my compliment."

I chuckle. "It kind of does." Reaching for a napkin, I clean the mess. When I look up, the stern stare is gone and she's looking at me sweetly.

"Tristan, you've done good with him. I'm so amazed. And I admire you so much."

Her kind voice, her good heart, together they unlock something in me. Maybe it's the seven layers of self-protective armor. Or possibly it's plain stubbornness.

"Thanks," I say, finally accepting what she's giving

me, emotion clogging my throat. "I appreciate it. I'd do anything for him."

Her smile is so soft, so endearing, that it nearly makes me forget I was *this close* to clasping her face on the stairs and growling, *Kiss me.*

Right now, she's the friend she's always been—warm, caring, loving.

She's everything she's ever been to me.

And I have to steer this conversation far away from warm fuzzies and mutual admiration. "So, what do I need to wear to homecoming?"

She wiggles a brow, going with my 180. "Depends if you want me to rip off your shirt."

God, yes. I pick up my taco and bite into the rest of it, putting off a response with a full mouth.

"But I think wear what you usually wear," she says.

"All I own are Henleys and jeans. Some sweatshirts. And the shirts I bought for the button experiment."

"You're not wearing a sweatshirt." Peering at my eyes like she's studying them, she hums, then says, "My vote is for a forest-green Henley. It's very you, so you'll feel good in it, and it'll also make your eyes pop even more."

I laugh. "You sound like you're talking to a customer."

"Is that so wrong? Besides, you would look good like that."

"Yeah?"

"You always look good, Tristan." There goes my heart again, skipping beats like the idiotic organ it is.

"I don't think I have one that color," I say, needing to segue to brass tacks. "I'm not even sure what forest green is."

She rolls her eyes. "I'll handle it. Don't think twice about it." She sets her chin in her hand. "But what should I wear?"

"I thought you were going as Marie Antoinette?"

"I was just playing around. But I do think I'll wear a dress."

"Color me shocked."

"Barrett will be so bummed I'm not in costume," she says with an aw-shucks snap of her fingers.

My mind latches onto Barrett's comments the other night. "I think he has a crush on you."

She scoffs, her answer emphatic. "He doesn't."

"How can you be so sure?"

"He just doesn't. He likes me in a friendly, big-sister way. The way you turn to the sister of a buddy."

"Some guys like the sisters of their buddies," I point out.

She shakes her head. "He doesn't think of me like that. His interests are elsewhere. Trust me, I'd know."

My eyebrows rise. I'm intrigued by her comment, curious if all men are that transparent to her. "How would you know?"

She nods, taking another bite. "Younger guys tend to give that stuff away easily." She gestures to her face.

"You can see it in their expressions, their eyes, their gestures."

Ah, that makes sense. "Do older guys do that too?"

She stops, studies me, then shakes her head. "No, they don't give away their feelings so easily."

I let out a breath I didn't realize I was holding.

* * *

After I walk her home and say goodbye on her steps, she yanks me in for one of those classic Peyton hugs.

When I'm this close to her, inhaling her scent, feeling her body, I wonder if I'm giving anything away.

If I'm transparent.

But then, what would I have to be transparent about? What I felt tonight is what any guy would feel when a pretty woman stripped down to nearly nothing. Just a normal bit of lust, that's all.

After we pull apart, she waggles her fingers goodbye. "See you Saturday, Fred. Isn't that your busiest day?"

"Of course it is. But I've hired good people, so I'm all set."

"Then I'll see you on Saturday. I'll be the woman wearing red."

The image of her in that bra I picked up the other day flashes before my eyes. Taunting, teasing.

It's just lust. It's just desire. Nothing more.

I can't act on it.

For so many reasons, but chief among them is this: I don't want to lose another person I love.

I care about her too much as a friend to risk what we've built. That's what matters.

When she reaches the door to her brownstone, I call out in my best friendly, sarcastic, buddy voice, "See you this weekend, Gingersnap."

I hope it fools her into thinking I only see her as a friend.

17

PEYTON

The Lingerie Devotee: Don't Try This at Home
Blog entry

The name says it all.

A lace plunge teddy.

And plunge I did.

I plunged to my butt. I plunged to my elbow. I plunged nearly all the way down the stairs.

Wait.

Is "plunge" one of those cringeworthy words?

Now that I write it over and over, I fear we might need to send "plunge" the way of "moist," "pucker," and "Uranus."

Let's not use words like "plunge" when referring to sexy lingerie, shall we agree?

So what if the makers of this satiny garment call it a

lace plunge teddy? I say we give it a new name. The lace V teddy, because it cuts a V down my neck, between my breasts, to the top of my belly button.

V indeed.

And last night, it gave me confidence. It helped me radiate desire, and it boosted my spirits.

But the thing is, asking a man to disrobe you while you walk up the stairs in heels is like trying to run the egg-and-spoon race while also carrying a wily cat in your arms and balancing a bucket of water on your head.

IT DOESN'T WORK.

Or, really, it works phenomenally well if your goal is to twist your ankle.

My handsome scene partner and I reenacted the staircase strip four times last night. Each time, we landed on our butts, elbows, hips, or the wrong side of our feet.

The problem is, you're *not* supposed to land. You're supposed to parade upstairs, looking sensual, shooting sexy-times eyes at your lover, and sashaying to Sade.

But where there's a will, there's a way.

We were determined to make this scene work, so we found a way. Or, rather, he did.

He took the lead, whispering naughty words and deeds in his smoky, gravelly voice as he followed me up the steps.

Then, when we reached the top step, he whisked off my dress.

In one bold, swift, commanding move.

Like a hero in a romance novel, casually, coolly dropping the fabric to the floor.

And my silky black clothes pooled by my feet as I stood wearing only heels and a teddy that exposed most of my flesh.

Most.

But not all.

Plenty was left to the imagination.

And that's why I say don't try the staircase shimmy at home. But *do* indulge in a piece of clothing that will make you feel adored when the one you want tugs everything else off you.

In short? Make this move your own.

Xoxo

The Lingerie Devotee

Find me at You Look Pretty Today on Madison Avenue

18

PEYTON

When I walk into Gin Joint on Friday night to see my girls, I check if I have toilet paper on my Jimmy Choos.

Nope.

Maybe a leaf fell into my hair? I brush a hand over my head as I make my way to the purple velvet couch Amy and Lola have commandeered in the center of the lounge.

With the way my two best friends stare at me, like I'm a giraffe walking backward, something has to be amiss.

I run my hands down my leopard-print skirt, then check my backside. "Do I have lint on my shirt? Dirt on my nose? A sign taped to my back that says I ate two whole chocolate bars for lunch? Because I swear, if Marley ratted me out about my midday Lulu's Chocolates scarf session, that girl is toast."

Amy blinks, holds up a stop-sign hand. "Wait. Your

dessert compartment is that big? It holds two chocolate bars?"

I sit next to her, crossing my legs, answering primly, "It wasn't my dessert compartment. It was my lunch compartment."

Lola bows. "I had no idea it was possible to eat two chocolate bars for lunch. I humble myself before you, O Great Chocolate Queen."

I pat her curls. "You may rise now, my subject." Taking a moment, I stare at them like they're crazy. "Guys! No, I didn't eat two chocolate bars." I lower my voice, cupping my hand to my mouth. "I had *one*. But seriously. Why are you staring at me with those you're-so-naughty eyes?"

Amy gently shoves my leg. "Because you are naughty. Ahem." She clears her throat, adopts a sultry tone. *"But do indulge in a piece of clothing that will make you feel adored when the one you want tugs everything else off you."*

I shrug as a waitress swings by and asks for my order. I eye Amy's drink.

"This one's called Last Word. It's delish," Amy says. "Get it."

"I'll have the same, thanks," I tell the woman, then return to my friends. "So, what's the issue with my blog?"

Lola blinks rapidly. "What's the issue? You just declared in a public forum that you want Tristan."

"No. No, that's not what I said." I jerk my head

back, shocked they'd leap to that conclusion. "I did not. I was writing about . . . "

But I don't entirely know how to fill in the blank. I was writing about whether romance novel scenes work. About walking up stairs. Was I writing about reenacting desire?

Or rekindling it?

Lola does know how to close the thought, it seems, since she jumps in. "You were writing about how you felt. With Tristan."

Her statement—bold, possibly true—rings like a gong.

And with it, a host of nerves descends on me. Nerves I haven't felt quite like this. Because this time, the nerves aren't about what I'm doing. They're about what I'm feeling.

Or, rather, what I can't let myself feel.

I recalibrate. "It was an experiment, and I was writing about it sort of as if I'm an everywoman. I was saying, as an everywoman, you want to feel desired when the guy, or gal, stares at you like they want to ravish you."

Amy points at me excitedly. "That's how he looked at you! Like he wanted to ravish you. I knew it. Called it."

She offers a high five to Lola, who smacks it.

"You're placing bets on how Tristan looked at me?"

They nod in unison, twin torturesses.

"And you guys are my friends, right? Just want to make sure."

"We are your people." Amy pats my knee. "Now, how did it feel when he stared at you like he wanted to eat you up like those chocolate bars?"

Decadent.

I wave a hand, wishing I could erase this conversation because it's treading on dangerous shores. "I wrote about it. It was an experiment. I wasn't saying he's the one I want."

Lola arches a brow, her expression shifting. "But do you? Do you want him?"

"Because it seems like maybe you do from those posts," Amy adds, a gentleness in her tone.

My throat hitches. My breath comes fast with the swell of rising emotions I do my best to deny. "I was just trying to capture a moment. To write broadly about how a woman might feel if she were in the shoes of a romance heroine."

"Did you feel like one?" Amy asks, all teasing stripped from her tone.

Did I?

Yes.

In my bones. In my heart. In my mind.

But I can't answer with words. If I speak, the reality might terrify me. I can only nod.

Lola inches closer. "Does that scare you?"

Yes.

But I don't want to give voice to the fear. I keep the question in my head a little longer, mulling it over, turning it this way and that. Maybe because I don't want to experience all this strange newness by myself, I manage to whisper, "So much," as the waitress brings me the drink.

"One Last Word for you," she declares.

Amy gestures to the waitress. "Add it to my tab."

The waitress leaves, and I pick up the glass.

"Why does it scare you?" Amy asks, returning to the question.

The question I need to figure out how to answer. "For so many reasons," I say, then I take a drink.

I don't want to list them all, because the list would occupy a sheet of paper so long it'd scroll out the door.

I knock back some of the beverage, savoring the clean, neat taste of the gin, then I turn the conversation in another direction. "The blog is working. Business has been picking up more than I could hope after only a few days," I say, rapping my knuckles on the metal table in front of me.

"That's great," Lola says with a smile.

I prattle on about the slight uptick in traffic to the store, and the comments on the blog itself, which is quickly picking up speed. "It's great to see the strategy working. Tristan said I should put more of myself into the blog, and that customers would connect with that."

Amy's eyebrows rise above her glasses. "I don't think your customers are the only ones connecting to the blog."

"I think *he* is too," Lola adds.

My brow creases. "Did he say something to you?"

Lola laughs, shaking her head. "He doesn't have to, Peyton. I've seen the way you two are together. How he makes you laugh, and how he pokes fun at you in the most deadpan way. And how you give it right back to him."

"Because we're friends. We always have been," I say.

"Right. That's true. But you weren't exactly hanging out with him all the time when you were with Gage."

"And that's why I'm glad that we *can* hang out again now. Like we did in college, and after college."

Lola takes a deep breath, as if she's steeling herself to say something hard. "I'm not trying to side with Captain Infidelity . . ." My shoulders tighten. I can hear the edge in her voice, the slice of tough love she's about to serve up. "But do you think maybe Gage was onto something when he didn't want you to spend time with Tristan?"

My jaw ticks. "I was faithful to Gage. I've been faithful to everyone I've been with. I would never cheat."

Lola squeezes my knee, but I shrink away.

She's insistent though. "Peyton, I know that."

"We know that," Amy adds. "You're a faithful person."

"I am," I insist. But why so strongly? It's nothing but the truth. "I was faithful mentally, emotionally, and physically in every way to everyone I've ever been with."

"Of course you were. But you're also an honest

person, and Gage knew you'd kissed Tristan. You told him about the kiss," Amy says.

"Yes, because otherwise I would have been keeping it a secret, and there was no reason for it to be a secret. I was honest with him about everything. Telling Gage I kissed Tristan was the right thing to do."

"Yes, it was. It absolutely was. And Gage is a total asshat," Lola says. "But he's also a human who was probably more jealous than he ever let on. So even if you weren't thinking of Tristan as boyfriend material when you were with Gage, you were certainly thinking of him that way once upon a time, weren't you? It wasn't just a random kiss in college, was it?"

I drop my head in my hands, the past crawling over me, digging its heel into my back.

Memories of college, of the times Tristan and I spent together before the dance, flicker in my mind. After he finished work, we'd meet for late-night study sessions for our history class, or we'd share notes for Spanish. On weekends, we'd go to the on-campus diner for milkshakes and fries, then salads the next day because we felt guilty about the fries. Sometimes we went out with our group of friends, and sometimes it was just us. He told me stories about teaching his brother how to make a pizza from scratch then showed me pictures of a young Barrett covered in tomato sauce and flour.

We played blackjack and made up new rules, and we read articles in *The Onion* out loud to each other in the snack bar, each doing our best to make the other laugh like a hyena.

We were friends.

Except for that one night.

I'd wanted more than that one night. I thought about him all through winter break, wondering, wanting.

Was he the one for me?

After his father passed away, we returned so seamlessly to friendship that it was as if the kiss had never happened. We never spoke of it. He gave no sign he wanted anything more.

But maybe Gage *was* right to be jealous of Tristan. Maybe it's normal to be jealous of any man your girlfriend has kissed.

I look up, seeing the patience in Amy's and Lola's eyes, pure friendship in their expressions.

"Yes, once upon a time, I wanted more," I admit.

A weight lifts from my shoulders.

But only for a moment. Then it crashes down heavier than before, a looming reminder of the risks.

Because that was in the past, and this is the present. "But there's too much at stake now," I continue. "And sometimes, chances slip by for a reason. I think we were meant to be friends. With friendship, I can't lose him. A quick romp, a one-night fling—those are too risky. Relationships can go up in flames. Look what happened to me."

I waggle my naked ring finger. "Three years with Gage and what do I have? Ten grand I poured into my store, and that's all well and good. But I loved him, and he hurt me. I care so deeply for Tristan that the thought of losing him makes me physically ill." I wrap my arms around my belly. "If I even tried to pursue something, acting on whatever this . . ." I gesture wildly, searching for words. "This *vibe* is, then what if it goes belly-up? What if it turns into the next bare ring finger?"

"He's not like Gage," Amy points out.

"But that's not even the issue," I add.

"I know," she says quietly. "You're not worried he'd cheat. You're worried you'd ruin the friendship if you let anything happen."

"Yes, because relationships are risky, but friendships are solid. Look at us now. We wouldn't be friends if we'd fallen into bed ten years ago. I need him in my life too much."

Amy raises her glass and says, "Let's drink to friendship."

Lola chimes in. "Friendship makes the world go round."

"Exactly. I don't want to lose you ladies ever, and I feel the same about Tristan. If I'm not going to sleep with you, I'm not going to sleep with him."

That decision felt right and solid when I said it to my girls. It's harder to remember when Tristan knocks on my door the next night.

19

TRISTAN

I spend the morning at the restaurant, managing inventory, paying bills, talking to suppliers.

My sous chef and I devise the specials, and I make small plates during lunch hour. When the rush dies down, I shift back to the office, finish some paperwork, and then pack up for the day, since my sous and the staff and crew can handle the night crowd.

Besides, I have a scene to attend.

And tonight's scene involves turning the tables on her.

I'm ripping off her panties, and she's going to wear red.

Red. Flipping red.

Which won't help my resistance.

Hence, the hour and a half I spend at the gym with the weights.

And on the treadmill.

And the elliptical too, for good measure.

As I leave, Linc walks in with Amy beside him. From the looks of it, she's showing him how her phone slides into the pocket of her bright-pink exercise pants.

She removes it with the showmanship of a magic trick. "See? We seriously need to plan a gift book about all the little things in life that bring joy, from pockets to hedgehogs to peeling a clementine in one strip," I hear her say.

Linc nods thoughtfully. "What about oranges though?"

"It's impossible to peel an orange in one go."

I cross their path, stopping to cut in on their conversation. "It's not impossible. Ever tried a mandarin?"

Amy blinks. "I stand corrected."

"Also, some grapefruits can be disrobed in one fell swoop," I say, then I realize I just walked into innuendo quicksand.

I wait for Amy to take the bait, to toss out something like "But how many licks does it take to disrobe a redhead wearing the sexiest pair of panties you've ever seen?"

But she doesn't say that. What's stranger is that she says nothing. Amy rarely takes the fifth.

Linc simply raises a brow. "Have fun tonight."

Amy smiles, shooting me a friendly grin. "May the force of romance novels be with you."

They walk past the weight machines, and I scratch my jaw. It's unlike the two of them to resist wordplay.

It's almost as if they have some sort of secret.

Or something they don't want to say.

But hell if I can figure out what it means.

Or if it means anything at all.

* * *

I return home, and as I walk into my building, my phone pings with a text.

Peyton: Are your teeth nice and sharp?

Tristan: Yes. I gnawed on a tree earlier today. Hung out with a pack of beavers. Chowed down.

Peyton: Excellent. So they're perfectly pointy.

I reach the stairwell and take the steps two by two as I answer her.

Tristan: Definitely. Let me guess—you want to test out a scene where the hero rips duct tape with his teeth before he hoists a couch on one shoulder?

Peyton: Yes. I want you to do lots of manly stuff like that.

Tristan: Manly stuff, check.

Peyton: Also, it turns out that not only does the hero in this book like to shred panties . . . he likes to shred them with his teeth.

I trip.

My phone flies out of my hand and skids across the concrete landing as I fall on the staircase, tumbling over my own feet.

My knee smarts, screaming from the impact. Glancing behind me, I see no one there to witness my stumble, and I breathe a huge sigh of relief.

Hell, that was more than a stumble.

That belongs on epic fails on YouTube. That should be a PSA not to text while walking up stairs.

Or down stairs.

I push up and grab my phone. Dragging my hand through my hair, I shake off the momentary pain, but I can't shake off the thought of tonight's task.

Testing the rip-ability of panties with my hands would have been challenging enough. A true feat of strength, but not an insurmountable one, since she'd be wearing the "bathing-suit-style birthday suit," her words. She said she planned to wear a thong under the lace panties I was supposed to tear off her.

What was I supposed to say to that?

Thanks, but no thanks?

My brain was shouting *hell yeah* to any and all of those options. Aloud, I'd kept it to a simple "Sure."

Now, she doesn't want me to rip her panties off with my hands. She wants me to use my teeth.

Which means my face will be *this close* to heaven.

I don't know if this is a gift from the angels or a temptation by the devil, but my money is on the latter, especially after she sends me a few hundred words from the scene.

I'm so screwed.

I push open the door to my floor, stride down the hall, and unlock my apartment.

Music assaults my ears, but in a good way.

A hip-hop song blasts across the apartment, which is filled with the scent of something yummy. Is that cookie dough? Or baked pretzels? Or both?

Whichever, the smell and the music take my mind off of devils and angels.

After shutting the door, I head into the kitchen. Barrett is laughing, his back to me, stirring batter in a mixing bowl and shaking his hips while Rachel sings into a spatula microphone.

Head back, eyes closed, she belts out some Adele-like harmony, layering onto the tune.

Barrett joins in, stirring and singing and laughing.

"Hey there."

Barrett swivels around, waves a spoon at me. Rachel beams, shouting, "Hi, Mr. Alexander!" over the song.

Barrett reaches for his phone, lowering the volume. "Yo."

I meet our guest's eyes. "Rachel, you don't have to call me Mr. Alexander."

"I do though. You're a mister! How are you, Mr. Alexander?" She flashes her bright smile at me, looking like a teenage Anna Kendrick, as Peyton once described her.

"Excellent. What are you two up to?"

"We're baking cookie dough pretzels, and then we're going to take them to some of the tech crew tonight," Barrett offers, his grin matching hers. Damn, he lights up when she's around—I'm talking Broadway-marquee wattage.

"Yeah, because the tech crew needs love too," Rachel says, offering a palm to high-five.

He smacks it, snickering, and they have an insider humor going on. Maybe he has manned up? I smile privately, hoping he'll have his heart's desire—the girl he adores.

Rachel returns to the batter, tossing a question over her shoulder. "And what are you up to, Mr. Alexander?"

"I'm going to see Peyton in a few," I say.

"Not dressed like that, I hope?" she asks.

I glance down at my basketball shorts and sweat-soaked T-shirt.

"Ladies don't like basketball shorts, don't you know that?" Barrett teases, flashing me an evil grin as he lobs my fashion advice back at me.

I pluck at the shirt. "I'm obviously not wearing this to see her."

Rachel wipes a flour-covered hand dramatically across her forehead. "Good. Because I was going to have to go all fashion police on you."

"And what exactly are you doing tonight with Miss Valencia?" Barrett asks oh so casually.

"Just hanging out."

They burst into matching peals of laughter.

Rachel points at me. "You're blushing, Mr. Alexander."

Ah, hell. Am I as red as a tomato? No way. "I'm not."

"Hey, handsome," Barrett says in a torch-singer tone. "Why don't you put on a corset and go see the one you want?"

I will never live this down.

I wave them off and head for my bathroom.

"Don't forget to wear something pretty, Mr. Alexander."

I shut the door. No wonder he likes her. She's just like him.

Thirty minutes later, I'm dressed and ready, wearing jeans and a Henley, my hair a little wet at the ends.

But am I truly ready?

Each session with Peyton is a new clue in an escape room, each mystery tougher than the last. Solve it and you can leave with your sanity intact. If you don't, time runs out while you dissolve into a puddle of lust on the floor.

But it's more than lust I feel for her.

So much more.

That's the twist I can't solve in this Peyton romance-novel-reenactment escape room.

How the hell am I going to handle being that close to her? What kind of superman human shield do I need to lock in place?

I pinch the bridge of my nose and remind myself that I've seen her in a bikini. I've seen pics of her in lingerie. Tonight I'm an actor, and I'm going to take home an Oscar.

On my way out, I find Barrett and Rachel huddled with his phone on the couch, taking selfies. Looks like they're messing around with filters, something I will never understand the allure of.

"Yes. Send that one of us," she says.

I clear my throat. "Hey. I'm going to head out. What are you two doing?"

"Just a group chat with the crew," Rachel says. "Eli and Chloe, and Maggie and Jacob."

"The ones you're taking the cookie pretzels to?"

Barrett taps his nose. "You catch on fast, Einstein."

I gesture to the door. "And on that note, I'm going to get out of here, which will sorely limit your targets for sarcasm, but I still wish you a good night."

Barrett winks. "I wish you a good night with your

homecoming date." He nods at Rachel. "He's taking Peyton to homecoming."

I'm about to fire back with *Well, are you taking Rachel?* when I remember—I'm the parent. Or the closest thing he has to one.

Barrett points a finger at me, making a circle. "What is tonight's test? Will she be testing how you smell? Because I can loan you my aftershave. It's pretty sex-ay."

Rachel grins. "Maybe you should do that thing in the movies where you run across a field of flowers and you catch her in your arms. Have you thought about that for a reenactment?"

I wave them off. "I'll make sure to let her know the flower field was your idea."

Barrett salutes me. "See you later. If you need cheesy pop music for that big moment, let us know."

"We'll make you a playlist. Maybe some Celine or Mariah," Rachel calls out as I leave.

"I'm all good," I say, then I get the hell out of the firing range of those two sarcasm monsters.

Their advice is good though. Not the field of flowers advice. But the *bring something* advice.

On the walk over, I pop into a bodega, grab a little gift, then use the cool fall air to clear my mind the rest of the way to her place.

This is an experiment.

Research.

That's all.

But when I reach her apartment and she opens the

door, all those reminders run, hop, skip, and jump away.

And it's not because of how she looks, though she's so damn pretty in a light-blue dress.

It's what she says.

"Listen to this voicemail a customer left for me." In one smooth move, she grabs my arm, tugs me inside, and hits play on her phone as the door closes.

Hi Peyton,

It's Sandra here! Just wanted to leave a little message! I stopped by your store the other day and picked up some new pj's. Ah, how I love my satin jammies—they're the perfect way to end the day. You were so helpful, aiding me in selecting just the right set. You remind me of Mimi. She always had time for every customer, talking to them, getting to know them. She'd be so proud of you, carrying on her legacy. And I know she'd be proud of your blog too. I can see where you get your spirit from!

P.S. You should stock knee pads for staircase use! It makes it so much more enjoyable! Helps with rug burn too!

See you soon!

. . .

Peyton sighs happily, brings her hand to her chest, then smiles. "Is it weird that I'm happy that she thinks my Mimi would be proud of me for selling undies well?"

I smile, shaking my head, my heart warming at how radiant she is over a message like this. The simplest things make her shine. "No. You have a connection with your grandmother. And you don't just do what you do to make a sale. You do it because it makes your customers feel better about themselves. You make them happy."

She points at me, doing a dance with her fingers. "See? You get my love of underwear."

Does she have any idea how much? "Yeah, I think I do."

"Also, you look . . ." She stops, and her eyes travel up and down my frame. "You look great."

The way she says it, it's as if she's stripped bare for me, like her voice holds the raw truth of her heart.

Three simple words. *You look great.*

They burrow into me, reminding me this is so much more than an experiment.

That's the big problem.

I hold up the bag I picked up on the way, needing to get out of the line of lust-fire. "I stopped at a store. The first crop of clementines are in. Did you know you can sometimes peel one in a single go?" I ask, making small talk as I cross the few feet into her kitchen.

"Yes. I love it when that happens. It's sort of like the satisfaction you get when you perfectly flip an egg or a pancake."

"Exactly. Want to try?"

She's right behind me in the kitchen, so close I can smell her body lotion. It's cherry blossom, and I'm going to need another coat of armor. Maybe there's a spare under the sink? In the hall closet?

Or possibly I can find it in the clementine trick. Yes, I'm sure my kitchen skills will solve this escape-room clue. Worth trying, at least.

"Not this second, because I have something for you," she says, waylaying my plan, and I spin around, surprised.

She's holding a gift bag with a silver bow tied around the handles. Because of course she is. Because that's what she does.

My heart dares to thump harder, and I have got to get it under control. I take the bag, untie the bow, and peer inside.

I smile when I see what she's gotten. "Forest green," I say, running my finger over the soft fabric.

"Take it out. Hold it up."

"Seriously?"

"Yes," she says, stomping her foot.

"Fine, fine." I tug the shirt from the bag, pretending to model it.

She nods approvingly. "Very you. Now you're all set for homecoming. And the clementines will go perfectly with my drink choice for tonight."

As I fold the shirt, I ask what's on tap.

She swivels around, grabs a bottle of tequila, and waggles it. "Shots."

Sounds like a good idea. Shots equal more armor.

She lines up two glasses, and I peel a clementine, all in one neat piece.

She whistles her appreciation as she pours the drinks, and we lift our glasses.

"What are we toasting to?" I ask, some ancient part of me hoping she'll say, *To us.*

She licks her lips, takes a breath, and seems to pause on the words. Then, with a rise of her chin, she declares, "To red lingerie and friendship."

That less-than-subtle hint is all I need to know.

Besides, it's precisely what I *should* drink to.

I down the tequila in two seconds, the fiery burn a stark and necessary reminder of reality.

I pour another shot and swallow it whole, then I grab a slice of clementine.

She finishes her drink, takes the fruit, and sets her phone in its stand. "I made a playlist. Mood music."

I hope it's not Chris Isaak again. I'm not sure my heart can handle that. "Metal music would be perfect," I say, dead serious.

With a roll of her eyes, she laughs and says she'll be right back.

As she leaves, Aerosmith's "I Don't Want to Miss A Thing" begins.

Well, that's not exactly Ozzy Osbourne.

Shoving my hand through my hair, I repeat her words while she's gone.

Lingerie and friendship.

That's what this is. That's what it should be. That's all she wants.

Now I know. Whatever I've been feeling these last few nights is one-sided. Like it's always been.

And it's time for this unrequited shit to end.

After her five scenes end in a few more days, I'm going to have to mix a drink that'll make me forget I ever had any feelings for her.

But I can't forget tonight.

Because when she returns a few minutes later, all the air rushes out of my lungs.

I can't think. I can't speak. I am on fire, burning alive.

Peyton, the woman I fell in love with ten years ago, wears a black satin robe that ends at her thighs.

Black heels raise her up a few inches.

And the lace of her bra strap peeks out on one side.

"I wore the red for you," she says, so softly, so faintly I'm not quite sure I heard her right.

I don't even know if it's a line from the novel. It doesn't feel familiar, but hell if I know anything anymore.

I laser in on the task, my slim-to-nil chance of beating the ticking clock.

"Do you want me to say the lines?" I ask as calmly as I can, but even so, the words come out like smoke.

"Yes." Hers sound like an invitation.

Lingerie and friendship.

I repeat it as I walk over to where she stands, poised against the wall.

"Did you wear this for me?" I fiddle with the satin ribbon at her waist, like the hero does.

"Just for you," she whispers.

Taking a deep breath, I untie the sash, the two sides of her robe falling open.

I shut my eyes briefly. I have to. She's so fucking beautiful.

When I open them, I half wish she'd changed into sweatpants. But she's the woman in red lace, with a bra that boosts her breasts, panties that should be worshipped, and a soft, supple body I want to have against mine.

I glance at the panties, noticing the lines for the tiny second-layer thong underneath. *Shame.* "These are pretty," I say, raising a brow, like the hero does. "Too bad they won't be on for long."

"Take them off," she murmurs, and her voice sounds different. Hotter, more sensual.

It's a trick. It's a tease. It's magic, that's all.

Don't be fooled.

I say what the hero says. "You know my favorite way to remove them."

A smile seems to tug at her lips. "That's what I want."

I kneel before her, and this—this is where I earn my Oscar for resistance. *I'd like to thank the Academy.*

Because, seriously? How the hell am I supposed to rip these off with my teeth without touching her? Would have been helpful for the hero to leave a step-by-step guide. Maybe a wiki or a how-to video.

Oh wait. He got to touch the heroine.

Lucky fucker.

I give it my best shot, dipping my face toward her, keenly aware of how ridiculous this is—I'm about to tear off her underwear for the sake of a blog.

Then walk away.

Must make light of this.

I glance up at Peyton and chomp my teeth, pretending I'm an animal about to devour its dinner.

But she doesn't laugh. The expression on her face is not one of amusement.

It's something else entirely.

Something I don't want to name.

With my arms at my sides, I bite at the top of her panties near her hip, and then briefly wonder what the hell to do with my hands.

"Put your hands on my ass," she says, like she can read my mind, or maybe my body language.

"It'll be easier that way," she adds.

"Right, easier," I murmur around the panties in my mouth, then slide my hands around her body, cupping her cheeks.

Holy fuck. She feels spectacular. Soft and smooth and so damn close.

Too close.

I'm losing my mind like this. I need to get out of this trap of desire, but it's a force of its own, shrouding me.

I try again, tugging at the lace, and she trembles the

slightest bit. I hear a tiny hitch of her breath, testing my resolve.

I need to just get this over with and leave.

I draw a deep breath, ready to yank with everything I have, but I freeze when I feel her touch my hair.

That's not in the script.

The way she threads her hands through my hair like a lover—that's not in the scene at all.

I let myself give a name to the way she looked at me moments ago.

She looked at me with arousal.

Now she's touching me the same way too.

20

PEYTON

There are reasons to resist crossing the line.

So many reasons.

And then there is *this*.

My best friend, on his knees, about to reenact an intimate scene.

Maybe I'll regret my actions in the morning.

Maybe I'll regret them in a few minutes.

But right now? With my playlist shifting to Janelle Monae and him looking at me with you're-so-beautiful in his eyes, I can't regret this feeling.

This wish.

This wild, powerful, almost painful desire.

I have to know what it's like to be touched by someone I trust. How it feels to be cherished.

And I know, without a doubt, he'll touch me that way.

I know, too, that I want Tristan desperately.

Maybe more than the woman in the book wants her man.

In this moment, I'm made entirely of emotion. Of desire. My skin tingles, and my body is awash with heat.

My heart stutters, longing for him.

I can't just playact this scene.

Or perhaps I simply don't want to.

I run my fingers through his hair, savoring the soft feel of his thick, dark strands.

"I wore the red for you," I say, repeating my words from earlier. *My words.* They're not in the scene. They're only mine, and they're wholly true. "I know you love red."

He stares up at me with so much intensity in his hazel eyes, so much desire. It's terrifying the way he looks at me. And wonderful too.

"I do. Love it so much," he says, his voice low and husky.

I shudder from the sheer magnitude of this moment. From the reality of what I'm about to do.

Jump.

"I know," I whisper, then I thread my fingers through his hair, curling them around his head, loving the feel of him. I guide him to my thigh, directing him.

He lets out a shuddery breath, then presses a ghost of a kiss on my bare leg.

I gasp.

The feel of his lips is extraordinary. The touch of his hands is utterly erotic. He shifts from cupping my ass cheeks to squeezing and kneading, bringing me closer.

And, like that, we cross the line of friendship.

We vault over it as he kisses my thigh, my hip, and moves up my belly. His lips travel across my skin, turning me liquid, transforming me into a molten woman.

He reaches my breasts, kissing the swell of one, then the other. When he arrives at my neck, his hands are on my waist, and his lips caress the hollow of my throat.

I shudder, murmuring, gasping all at once.

I'm in another realm, where passion rules the night and choices narrow to one—the choice is *touch*.

He kisses my neck, my jaw, the shell of my ear, his trim beard rasping deliciously across my skin. Then he stops, plants his palms on the wall behind me, and meets my eyes. I've never seen someone look at me the way he does. The intensity, the desire is almost too much.

"Kiss me," I whisper, desperation coloring my tone.

"I want to kiss you all night long," he says. Then his lips meet mine, and I am lost—completely lost in the sensation.

In the brush of his lips, the feel of his body, the power of his kiss.

He's not soft or gentle. He's all man, all hunger, and he kisses me like I'm the most succulent dish he's ever tasted. He seals his mouth to mine like he owns me, like he already knows the taste of me.

Like he wants me with a wild desperation.

Looping my hands into his hair again, I thread my fingers through the strands, playing with the ends.

He sighs against my mouth, his body trembling, and I smile inside, knowing he likes how I touch him.

I want him to. I want him to like everything I do. To feel everything I feel. Lowering his right hand, he cups my jaw, brushing his thumb over my chin as he kisses me.

Somehow this takes the kiss even higher, makes it even hotter. It's like he's talking with his hands, saying how much he needs me.

I need him just as much.

But I need more than kissing.

So much more.

I break the kiss, grinning as I reach for his hand. He's quiet, letting me lead. I swallow roughly, then guide his hand down my body. He shudders as I go, and we blaze a trail down my breasts and over my belly. When we reach the top of my panties, he takes over, sliding his hand between my legs.

"Oh hell," he groans, his eyes squeezing shut as he feels my wetness through the lace, and the little thong too.

His fingers trace lines over me, then he seems to collect himself, issuing a command. "Turn around."

"Against the wall?"

"Yes."

I do as I'm told, thrilling at the confidence in his voice, the dirty need.

I turn, and as I go, I slide off the robe so I'm only in my red lace.

"God, yes. You're so fucking incredible," he says, then presses his big body against my back.

I gasp when I feel the outline of his erection, thick and insistent.

He slides my hands up the wall, above my head, holding them there with one hand. Then his other arm glides around my body, over my waist and down, his fingers dipping inside my panties, touching me while his lips press against my neck again.

Twin sensations—his fingers gliding between my legs, his lips traveling across my neck.

I moan and writhe, wriggling against his hands, arching into his lips.

He plays with me, rubbing and touching me where I need him most, winding me up, driving me wild.

"You feel spectacular," he growls, and I do feel that way—because of him. Because of how he touches me. "You're so fucking soft. So wet."

I can't even answer. I don't know what to say. All I can say is *"Yes"* as he strokes and thrusts and sends me toward the edge.

His hungry mouth consumes me, kissing my neck fiercely, reverently, as he fucks me with his fingers.

All these sensations collide in a tightening in my belly, an exquisite tension in my legs. Then I break, gasping and crying.

"Oh God, oh God, yes. Oh my God."

I fall apart with him, regretting nothing. Only wanting more.

When I come down from the high, I turn around, my legs like jelly, my brain high on dopamine. I clasp his cheek. "Will you please take me to bed now?"

His grin is wicked, and I don't ever want to forget the way he's looking at me right this second. "I will."

It sounds like the answer to a prayer.

21

PEYTON

I don't know if this is a vivid dream or heightened reality.

Reality has never felt as blissful, as unexpected, as it does when I stand in front of my king-size bed as Tristan lifts a hand to my chest, his fingers featherlight as he flicks open the front clasp on my bra.

I release a shuddering breath.

I'm getting naked for my friend.

He's stripping me down to nothing.

I want this so badly, and I'm terrified at the same time.

What does this mean? Where do we go from here?

But I *need* what's next.

Need it more than chocolate and lace.

When my bra falls open, my breasts revealed to him, a gust of breath rushes from his lips.

"You're so stunning," he whispers, his voice rough

as gravel and yet dusted in honey at the same damn time. Like he can't believe he's looking at me like this.

But I feel the same about him.

I can't quite fathom that this strong, gorgeous man who I desperately wanted years ago is undressing me. For several surreal seconds, I'm sure I'm living a fantasy.

"I like the way you look at me," I say, needing to be sure this is real life, and holy hell, that felt good to say.

He shakes his head, like this is all a dream to him too. He cups my breasts, and we both groan at the same time.

He fondles them but doesn't linger long. On a fast track for total nudity, his hands skate down my stomach and slip into my panties. He slides them, and the thong, down my legs, his breath hitching as I'm revealed.

Shamelessly, he gazes up and down my body as he helps me step out of the lace.

When he rises, he glides a hand around to my ass, dips his mouth to my neck, and whispers, "Let's leave your shoes on."

A tremble radiates through me. "Better to wrap around your hips that way."

He jerks back, stares at me, then quirks his lips. "You dirty woman." He presses a kiss to my jaw. "You can leave your shoes on with me anytime, you dirty, beautiful, fucking sexy woman."

Woman.

He calls me "woman," not "girl."

And that turns me on even more.

But what would make me molten is seeing him.

I play with the waistband of his shirt. "My turn to strip you."

"Don't let me hold you back." His tone shifts to playful, his eyes twinkling with mischief. But the lightness fades once more as I lift his shirt, raising it over his head and dropping it to the floor.

The enormity of this choice echoes in my mind and sears in my brain. I'm doing this. *We're* doing this.

Damn the consequences.

My eager hands are ahead of my mind, my fingers trailing down the firm expanse of his chest, playing with the most delicious smattering of hair. Trembling, I continue my travels, an explorer traversing a new land.

He seems to sense I need this—this moment—to revel in the brand-new territory, to discover my best friend in this new way. He's still as stone, letting me take this journey, like a cat in a new apartment, checking out every nook and corner.

The V of his abs. The grooves in his flat stomach. The happy trail that leads to where I want to be.

My fingers wander across the planes of his belly as I trace every carved inch of him, mesmerized by his body. Lifting my chin, I meet his gaze. Desire has darkened his eyes once more. His hazel irises shimmer with lust—a lust that heats me up.

"You're kind of hard everywhere," I whisper, then shake my head, correcting myself. I'm so lost in touching him that I can't speak properly. "Not *kind of*. You *are*," I emphasize, moving my hands to his arms, running them up his toned forearms to his biceps.

He's no longer a statue. He reaches for my waist, jerking my body close to his, my skin against his half-dressed frame. "Yes, I'm hard everywhere, Peyton. *Everywhere.*"

As close as he holds me, my hip is the lucky recipient of the evidence, and I feel just how much he wants me. I shudder, my voice barely a whisper as I say, "I better finish getting you undressed."

"Yes, you better."

I nibble on the corner of my lip, both insanely aroused by and slightly nervous about what we're doing. Somewhere in the back of my mind, or perhaps it's in the front, I'm acutely aware I should say something before we do the deed. The requisite *are we okay with this* check-in.

Hey, Tristan. Real quick. We won't let sex ruin our friendship, right?

'Course not. Friends with benefits sounds cool.

Awesome. I thought so too. Let me just get these pesky clothes off you right now.

But I don't want to lose the intensity of this moment. It's too perfect. Too wonderful in its own right.

Besides, of course we're okay with this. We can handle this.

And I want to keep experiencing all the wonder of undressing him.

I unbutton his jeans, unzip them, and push them over his hips.

He helps me along, kicking off his shoes and shedding his jeans, until he's down to only black boxer briefs that hide nothing. My mouth waters, and desire flickers through me like strobe lights in a disco.

I can't wait.

I need him.

Need *this*.

I strip off his boxers, and my lips part in admiration and desire when his cock springs free. He's beautiful. His cock is a work of art, a sculpture worthy of a museum exhibit.

I don't even know what to say as I stare at him in the flesh, drinking in his strong, powerful body, his thick, hard length.

Words feel foreign. The only language I know is sensation.

I wrap a hand around his hard shaft, hot and pulsing in my palm. As soon as I touch him, he exhales sharply, like he's been holding his breath forever.

Like I felt when he touched me.

The sound reassures me that he's in this too, every step of the way.

I ache exquisitely as I stroke him, making me want him more and more. I search for words, something to anchor me to this moment. "I kind of can't believe this is what you look like," I say, as speech comes to me at last.

He blinks, like he's trying to focus, trying to concentrate on answering me as I grip the steel of his erection. He rocks the slightest bit into my hand, need written on his face like a headline. "What do you mean?" he rasps out.

"All this time, all these years. And look at you," I say, staring unabashedly.

He swallows, his eyes locking with mine. "And what do you see, Peyton?"

What do I see?

More than I bargained for.

More than I ever expected.

I see trust and sex and beauty and friendship. I feel fear and desire and unfettered excitement. And I see *him*. The way I wanted to ten years ago.

"You're beautiful," I whisper, emotion tightening my throat. "Everywhere. And I want you now."

In one swift move, I'm on my back, legs spread, knees open, heels digging into my peach comforter. Tristan crawls over me, pinning my wrists at my sides. "Say it again," he commands, rough and gravelly.

"Which part?" I ask, arching my body, aching for him. A pulse beats insistently between my legs, and he's going to need to put me out of my misery soon.

"The last part," he says, lowering himself so his hard cock rubs against my belly.

"I want you," I say, gasping, desperate now. "I want you so much."

His jaw ticks, and he breathes out hard. "You have no idea."

"No idea what?"

He doesn't answer. Instead, he lets go of my wrists and rises to his knees, his eyes scanning the floor. "Need my wallet. Need a condom."

But I have another idea. "Tristan," I say, insistent, pushing up on my elbows. "I've been tested. Since my last relationship. I'm clean, and I'm on protection."

"Oh, fuck." He drags a hand through his hair like I've said both the best and the worst thing in the world.

"What's wrong?" I don't want to ruin the mood. I reach up to his face, cupping his cheek. "Did I say something wrong?"

He turns his face to my hand, kissing my palm, soft and tender. "No. You didn't say a thing wrong. And I'm clean too. I've been tested. I just don't know how the fuck I'm going to last inside you like that."

A smile spreads slow and easy on my face, and all my anxieties sashay out of the room. With my hand on his face, I pull him back down to me. "I guess we should try, then, and see."

He flashes me a wolfish grin. "I'll give it my best shot." He raises my arms again. "I love the way you look like this. Can you hold on to the headboard so I can fuck you like this?"

Can I? With fucking pleasure. I scoot up and reach for the headboard, gripping it.

He's on top of me, cock bobbing, parking his knees on either side of my hips, his hands sliding up my waist, over my breasts, to my neck. "Do you have any idea how gorgeous you look? How beautiful you are? You're so fucking stunning in every way, but especially like this."

My skin is sizzling. All the nerve endings in my body are unraveling. Pleasure consumes my every cell and he's not even inside me. He's simply praising me, and I could luxuriate in this attention all night long.

He lowers his face to my breasts and brushes a kiss between them, then more down my belly. "Your body . . .You need to be worshipped. I need to kiss every inch of you."

I want that. Desperately. I want to feel him adore me with his mouth, his tongue, his lips.

But I need to be filled right now.

I need to be fucked.

My eyes float closed, and I lift my hips. "Worship me tomorrow. Fuck me tonight."

The sound he makes is carnal and obscene. Like a wild animal.

And it thrills me, sending a wave of anticipation through my body. His hands slide between my legs, and he parts my thighs wider, settling between them. I open my eyes to see him running a hand down his hard shaft, then rubbing the head against my wetness.

My back bows.

His entire body shudders.

We are a feedback loop, and it's intoxicating.

He groans. I moan.

He shakes his head, like he can't believe this is happening. "I want you so fucking much."

Then he slides inside me, and I'm so wet, so ready, that he's all the way in me in seconds.

"Oh God," I murmur as I feel him fill me completely. Tingles spread everywhere, a rush of heat floods my body, and I don't want to hold on to the headboard anymore.

I want to touch him.

My hands fly to his chest, clutching him for dear life.

He doesn't move for a few seconds. Clenching his jaw, he closes his eyes. Then he opens them, meeting my gaze.

"I want this to be so good for you," he says, and there's pure honesty in his words, an admission in the middle of all this heat and need. He lowers his chest to mine.

I wrap my legs around him, hooking my high-heeled feet together over his firm butt. "It already is," I whisper as I lift my hands, thread them through his hair, and bring his face to mine, his stubble against my cheek.

He groans my name, some kind of plaintive wish to the universe as he starts to move in me with slow, unhurried thrusts.

The feel of him, the weight of him, the way he reaches for my thigh with one hand, angles me more open, is all so wickedly new and utterly wonderful.

I'm discovering a whole new side to my best friend tonight.

An erotic, seductive side.

A vulnerable, tender side.

With his palms planted by my face, he finds the most delicious rhythm, thrusting deep then stroking back, nearly pulling out before he drives back into me, right where I want him. *That* spot. Pleasure cascades through me, and I feel boneless as he fucks me, swiveling his hips, taking his sweet, fantastic time, and hitting the mark with every thrust.

He grins at me like he has a secret. "I'm going to make you come so fucking hard," he says, and I light up like a pinball machine.

Those words.

His intensity.

"Yes, please, yes," I say, dragging my nails down his back. "Make me come, Tristan."

"Like you did against the wall," he continues, his voice as ruthless as his desire. He rocks into me as tension grips my core.

"Yes, do it again," I urge.

"Love it when you come for me. I want to make you come so hard you lose your mind with pleasure," he says, and his filthy words flip the switch in me.

He has a dirty side too.

I never knew he was a dirty talker. How could I? The private knowledge thrills me, my body tightening, pleasure coiling in my belly. The ecstatic torture expands as I hover so damn close to the edge of release.

"Oh God, Tristan," I moan, lifting my hips closer, my head falling back on the pillow, my body taking over as I go wild beneath him, bucking. "I'm coming. Coming again."

One. Deep. *Thrust.*

And I am over the edge, tumbling into ecstasy as he praises me. "So fucking beautiful, so fucking perfect, love it when you come, love it so damn much."

His words merge into his groans and his pumps, the thrusts of his cock deep inside me as he fucks me to his own oblivion.

Then he fills me, his cock twitching, his body collapsing on me, his pulse racing so fast, I can feel it under his skin as my hands roam his frame.

We're both quiet for a minute. Our slowing breaths and the soft music from the other room are the only sounds.

Soon, our breathing slows. But I can't stop touching him. I want to worship him too.

I want to have him again and again.

And I hope, dear God, I hope that he wants all the same things I do.

When he slips away to the bathroom, grabs a washcloth, and cleans me up, I nearly cry. It's such a tender, sweet gesture. It's one I've never experienced from a man.

He sets the towel on the floor, returns to bed, and wraps an arm around my waist. Nuzzling me, he kisses my neck, then whispers, "I need to go soon."

That's not what I wanted to hear.

22

TRISTAN

The last thing I want on earth is to leave her.

But I have to.

Besides, leaving is easier.

If I stay, I'll curl up with her all night long, wrap her in my arms, and tell her she has my heart in her hands.

And what if she doesn't want me to spend the night?

I can't deal with any form of rejection this second.

Nor can I deal with a conversation about what this is or isn't. I'm not sure I want to have *any* conversation. Because I don't know what the hell tonight means for her. I've got no clue what we're doing or what she wants. But I can't handle hearing anything hard right now, anything that would slice my heart in half.

She has the power to destroy me, and I can't afford destruction. I have a business, a family, responsibilities.

I don't want to put my heart through that wringer again when I have to deal with life head-on every damn day.

Besides, I don't know if she chose me tonight, or if circumstance did. Because in the past, I've never been the guy she chooses.

That's why I need to leave.

Plus, I actually do have to go, even though I want so much more of her. I want her over and over.

"You have to go?" She scoots up in bed, sitting, wrapping her arms around her stomach.

I grab my boxers, tug them on. "Barrett will be home by midnight. Well, he'd better be. Curfew and all."

"Oh, right," she says, blinking, nodding. "Of course. You need to be home when he returns."

"I do." I love that she doesn't ask why, that she simply gets it. Sure, Barrett's a senior in high school and he can take care of himself. But I don't want him coming home to an empty house. That's not how I'm raising him—to fend for himself and set his own rules. I need to set an example for him of how to be a man, and this man has a responsibility.

To be home when his kid brother returns.

She slides out of bed, searching for her clothes. She yanks open a drawer in her bureau and pulls on a long T-shirt. But when she turns, and I see the panicked look in her eyes, it cuts me to the core. It reminds me of how she looked when she came to my restaurant after she found Gage in bed with another woman.

Devastated.

My heart lurches, and I grab her arm, spinning her around. "Peyton," I say, and it's the most desperate her name has ever sounded on my tongue. "Tonight was . . ."

A revelation?

Ten years in the making?

The most intense night I've ever had, and I don't want to let you go?

She presses her lips together, like she's holding in all her words too, all her feelings.

"Tonight was incredible," I continue, admitting some truth. "You're incredible." I draw her close, plant a kiss on her forehead. But she's tight and tense, and I fear I've done the wrong thing. Does she think this is a one-night stand for me? Is it for her?

But how can it be anything else?

Still, *one-night stand* doesn't feel like the right term for what just happened. Only, I don't have a clue what category to put this evening in.

I pull back, needing to reassure her of something that won't rip me to shreds. "You mean the world to me," I say, trying that on for size.

She nods, her shoulders shaking slightly. Her lip quivers. "But . . .? It sounds like there's a *but* in that sentence."

"But nothing. But everything." I cup her chin, wanting her to know what she means to me, how I can't stand the thought of her vacating my life. "I don't want to lose you. I don't want to lose our friendship."

"So we're still friends?" she asks, tentative.

"Of course. We better be."

"And we just do what? Put that behind us?" She flaps her hand toward the bed.

Oh, how I wish I could read her mind. That'd come in real handy right now. I cast about for something, anything, to save myself, to save us. "We don't have to put it behind us," I say, testing that option, as my brain tries to figure out what the hell we do next. Wind back the clock? Or spring forward into more sex? More experiments? I don't want to get hurt, but I'm dying for more of her. Once was not enough. Because, hell, this isn't a one-night stand for me.

"And if we don't put it behind us, we'd put it in front of us?" she asks, her eyes full of questions.

Yes. All the way in front of us, forever and fucking ever.

But that wayward thought stays locked up. "The way I see it is you have two more scenarios to play out," I say, because maybe *that's* the way to navigate through what this is—focus on the research. Yes, this new twist in the experiment is how I can have a little more of her for now, and still have her friendship when it ends. Because it *will* end. That's a fact of life.

She lifts a brow, intrigued, it seems. "What are you saying? That you want to try more scenes?" The words come out measured, but less awkward. We're returning to common ground.

I try to keep the mood light, hoping that works. "I don't think we're quite done, are we? I bet the book doesn't end with panty shredding."

Her lips twitch, as if she's holding in a grin. "Or panty shredding that led to sex."

"To amazing sex," I correct.

She shakes her head, tsking. "No, Tristan. It was earth-shattering sex."

"I stand corrected. Happily corrected." I square my shoulders, pride thrumming through me. "Maybe we should make sure some of the other scenes work too? And that they're just as toe-curling?"

She licks her lips, lifts her chin, then waves a hand, erasing the awkwardness. "Exactly. This doesn't have to change anything. I mean, c'mon," she says, nudging me with her elbow. "We kissed before, and we're still friends. We can totally screw and still be friends, right?"

And that's a nick to my heart, a small cut with the friends-with-benefits knife. But I can stanch the bleeding. Been there, done that, have the T-shirt.

Besides, I *do* want to be friends.

Always.

"Peyton, we're friends. Nothing is going to change that."

"Not even a couple experiments, right? And maybe we just needed to get that out of our systems?" Her tone is lighter now. Gone is the trembling lip, the knot of emotions. Maybe I imagined them.

"Considering it was ten years in the making, we might need to get it out of our systems more than once."

Her eyebrows wiggle. "Good point. Once for every three point three three years?"

I laugh to cover up the hole in my heart. "So, two more experiments and we're all clear?"

She taps her chin, like she's deep in thought. "Sounds about right."

Sounds like all I'll get.

And since I'm still starving, I'll take what I can get for now. I'll take one more kiss for the road too. I move in closer, cup her cheeks, and kiss her, trying to tell her with my lips all the things I can't and won't say.

I want so much more of you.

Once will never be enough.

Don't break my heart.

As my lips sweep over hers, she melts against me, kissing me back like she's saying all the same things.

But I'm probably just imagining it.

When I break the kiss, I make my best effort to zoom in on the task at hand. "So, doctor of romance novels, what tests are we running next?"

Maybe I've finally said the right thing, because she smiles at me, all flirty and coy again. "I have two things in mind."

"Do tell."

She stands on tiptoes, whispers in my ear, and I groan as the flash of images in my mind turns wildly pornographic.

"Same time tomorrow?" she asks.

"Yes." I turn away from her, grab my jeans and shirt, and get dressed.

She taps on my shoulder, looking like a naughty vixen. "But we didn't finish tonight's test. I know you need to go, but this is all in the name of romance science."

"Science is cool," I say as she scurries to her bureau, grabs a pair of lacy panties, and pulls them on. She tugs up her shirt, showing me a sexy pair of skimpy black panties. My dick jolts back to skyscraper levels.

"I love science," I say as she leans against the wall.

I stalk over to her, get down on my knees, grab her ass, and bite into the waistband of her panties. I yank them off in one move, as she yelps from the tear of the fabric.

I stare at the lace tatters on the floor, and then at her face wearing an expression of utter delight.

She snaps a photo of the carnage for her blog.

But when I leave, I keep thinking the lace won't be the only thing ripped to pieces when this experiment runs its course.

23

PEYTON

The Lingerie Devotee: Definitely Do This at Home
Blog entry

I can't believe I am writing this.

I feel like such a traitor.

An utter turncoat to all I hold dear in the world of lingerie. But I suppose I must do what all good bloggers do at some point.

Come clean.

It is my turn now to confess, and as much as I should hang my head in shame, I refuse to.

Because, ladies and gents, having your lover tear off your panties with his teeth is exquisitely erotic.

Even if it breaks my heart to see this little darling in shreds. These lacy numbers are delicate. Luckily I held up intact, without a tear or a scratch. But they didn't. See? Look what became of my sexy black lace panties.

How could I do this to them?

Yet there is something deliciously carnal in this scenario. It's animalistic in a way—tearing off someone's underthings with your bare teeth. And that's what works about the scene. Sure, it can be a bit camp if you let it. But if you set the mood, play the right music, and wear something sensual, then you just might find yourself aroused in all new ways.

Now, to be clear, I'm *not* simply saying this so you'll come to my shop and buy more panties.

I'm saying this because I want you to feel as good as I felt last night.

Everyone should feel as good as I felt. Last night was the pinnacle of sensations.

And if you decide to reenact this particular scene, do follow this piece of advice: *commit.*

Have your lover get on his knees, grab your rear, and then treat your panties like a piece of steak.

Trust me on this.

Because chances are, your pleasure won't end there. It'll last all night long.

Xoxo

The Lingerie Devotee

Find me at You Look Pretty Today on Madison Avenue

24

PEYTON

I toss the birdie into the air, raise my racket, and serve it over the net. It soars. My mom lunges for it, smacks it back. I dive for the prize, whacking it underhand and up over the net again.

Fast and furious as always, she reaches for it and lobs it to me.

Back and forth we go for another several minutes until she misses.

I thrust my arms in the air. "Badminton champion in da house!"

She rolls her green eyes. "Yes, as a former high school badminton winner, you should take pride that you can beat your fifty-five-year-old mother."

I tut her. "Mom. You're fifty-six."

She swats me on the butt with her racket. "And there are ten more spankings where that came from if you say my age again."

"Oh please, you don't look a day over fifty-five."

Her racket connects with my rear again as we leave the badminton court, wishing good luck to the next pair ready to tackle the sport.

"You are a most impudent child," she says.

"I'm the worst." I shrug happily. Because I am happy. Happily counting down the hours till I see Tristan again.

Six hours and fifteen minutes. Tonight can't arrive soon enough, but at the same time, I'm more wary than I was before. Because I don't know where we stand. I couldn't read him, couldn't tell what he wanted, if he was feeling the same new and wondrous connection I was.

Does he only want to be friends with benefits? Friends who needed to get a little lust out of their systems?

Part of me fervently wishes he felt more. But anything more is too risky, so I shouldn't even contemplate such possibilities.

"You okay? You drifted off there," Mom asks, breaking my reverie as we exit the badminton club.

"Of course," I say, quickly collecting my thoughts. "Just thinking about an order I placed this morning. For a second, I thought I forgot something in it," I say, fashioning a cover-up for my wandering mind.

"Is business going well with this new blog series? I know it's early days, but can you tell?"

"There is definitely an uptick in sales," I say with a smile as we head to our favorite cafe for Sunday lunch. "It definitely seems to be helping bring a little more attention to the shop. Even Jay and his wife are getting into it," I say, mentioning my brother.

"Your brother is wearing lingerie now? To each his own."

I laugh. "Who knows? But check out this text from him."

Jay: In case you're wondering, the guy who placed the order for three new bustiers this morning was me.

Peyton: You're going to look so pretty in that leopard print one especially.

Jay: Thanks. I was hoping it'd match my skin tone.

Jay: Also, they're for Holly.

Peyton: Yeah, I figured. What with them being a petite and all. Unless you planned to wear the bustier on your leg.

Jay: Make that your next blog post. Unusual uses for lingerie.

Peyton: Maybe *you* should write it for me.

Jay: I'll have it to you this evening. No photos though.

Peyton: Consider that a general rule of thumb for you, dear brother of mine.

Jay: Duly noted. Also, rush shipping please. As in overnight.

Peyton: They're already with Fedex. Good luck making babies!

Jay: Was it that obvious?

Peyton: Yes.

I close the text app. "Maybe you'll have grandkids soon, thanks to my blog."

She gazes heavenward and clasps her hands. "Please let my daughter's blog inspire my son to give me grandkids to spoil." Then she looks to me. "I'm glad the blog is working so well. It's hard to look away from it, after all. You're really putting it all out there."

I turn to meet her gaze as we reach the next block, curious what she means. "I am?"

"Yes, it's incredibly open and honest. Readers and customers are connecting with that, I imagine." She squeezes my shoulder. "I have to wonder if Tristan is too. He must be."

I tense. "How *should* he connect with it?"

She stops outside the cafe. "How do you want him to connect with it? That's the question." Her eyes lock with mine, overwritten with motherly wisdom.

I swallow roughly. "Mom . . . is it obvious?"

She smiles softly, petting my hair. "That you have feelings for him?"

I wince, then admit the truth, since she's seen through me already. "Yes."

"Oh, sweetheart." She wraps an arm around me and tugs me close. "It's obvious to me because I know you so well. I know who you are, what you want, what you need."

"And what is that?" I whisper.

"You want love. Great, beautiful, soul-searing love."

"Mom, stop," I say, as my heart catches in my throat. "That's too much."

She runs her fingers down my cheek. "You've always wanted that. And you've always trusted so easily. That's why it hurt so much when Gage showed his true colors—because you did love him. You did trust him. And he broke everything that mattered to you."

"He did." But my voice doesn't wobble this time because Gage is in the past. "But I'm over him. I've completely moved on."

"I can tell completely," she says with that sage look only a mom can give.

"How can you tell?"

"Because you're falling for your best guy friend, and anyone who knows you the slightest bit can see it."

I freeze as cymbals clang in my ears. As she bangs

the gong. I could deny it. I could backpedal. But I am cellophane to her, and always have been.

"How?" I press. "How is it obvious?"

She looks to the blue sky, then recites my own words. *"I'm saying this because I want you to feel as good as I felt last night. Everyone should feel as good as I felt. Last night was the pinnacle . . ."*

"You can't just quote me back to me."

"But I can, and I did."

"That was about—" I cut myself off before I say "sex" because I can't just admit to my mom that we had sex.

She laughs deeply. "Wait! Do you think I couldn't read between the lines? Sweetheart, I know you slept with him."

My jaw drops, and I am the definition of aghast. "Mom!"

She waves off my outrage. "I don't know that everyone else could tell you have feelings for him. But it seemed obvious to me."

"It did?" I ask, worry striking a chord in my heart. Could he tell? "Do you think he knows?"

"I'm not sure. Men don't always see what women see. And certainly not what mothers see. But I know you, and I've seen you with him. Like I said, there's a vibe." She pauses, searches my face. "But what did you think would happen when you decided to experiment like this with a man who's longed for you for a long while?"

I jerk my head, like she's speaking in limericks. "*Longed for* me?"

She sighs. "Peyton. You two—you have this thing."

I shake my head, denying, vehemently denying. "It's just chemistry, that's all. He doesn't want more. He said as much last night," I say, recalling the punch to the heart at his words. *You mean the world to me. I don't want to lose you. I don't want to lose our friendship.*

That's what matters most to him—keeping the status quo.

And it matters to me.

"And I don't want to lose him," I continue. "Mom, don't you see? There's too much at stake."

She takes a deep breath, nodding. "What are you going to do, then? Stop these experiments?"

I glance away. "Yes, soon."

She chuckles. "After you sleep with him again?"

I cover my ears. "Mom, stop talking about sex."

She removes my hands from the sides of my head, laughing. "Sweetheart, be careful. Or be bold. But you can't have both."

But she's wrong. I can be bold *and* I can be cautious. I know how to protect my heart, and it's by using my head. Last night, Tristan and I set the boundaries for our explorations. We picked an end date. We decided on the agenda.

We used our heads.

There.

Besides, we both want the same thing—to come out on the other side the way we started.

I repeat my mantra in my head: *Friendship and lingerie. Lingerie and friendship.*

After we finish lunch, I say goodbye, then head to WildCare where I volunteer, helping them with their mission to rehab injured birds and other wildlife. As I clean the facility, I compose a series of text messages in my head to Amy, smiling to myself as I devise ways to needle her and wind her up.

Texting Amy will be a fantastic way to pass the time this afternoon.

When I'm done, I walk through the park, tapping out a message to her.

Peyton: Hey, girl! You know that bathing suit I was going to wear to test out bathtub sex?

Amy: The royal-blue bikini with the white stripe? That's ghost-pepper hot, so be careful. You might ignite flames in the tub. Best for me to bring you a black Speedo and a bathing cap. Wait. You'll still look good in a Speedo, you mermaid. New plan—I'm going to bring you one of those full-body bathing suits they wore in those old-timey shots.

Peyton: I'm wearing something besides a bathing suit tonight.

Amy: *waits with bated breath* *stares at phone* *googles waterproof clothing options* *decides a rain slicker that goes to your ankles is what you mean*

Peyton: Nothing. I'm wearing nothing.

Three, two . . .

And before I can count down to one, my phone rings.

"Explain yourself, and leave no dirty stone unturned. Must know everything," she demands as I walk along the picturesque Terrace Bridge in the middle of the park, enjoying the early golds and bright reds of fall.

I smile, delighting in the memories of last night that are still wildly vivid. "We *might* have moved on to a new style of testing. Call it more hands-on research."

She shrieks. "Where are you? I need to see you. I need to see your face as you share every gloriously filthy detail with me."

"In the park."

"What side?"

"Why? Are you going to triangulate me?"

"Yes. I bet you're heading home after WildCare. I'm on the east side. I'll meet you at that cake shop I like on Park Avenue. Be there in fifteen minutes, ready to divulge every salacious detail."

"Cake shop you like? Ames, you're going to need to narrow it down. You like every cake shop."

"I am very picky with cake, and you know it. Meet me at the newest Sunshine Bakery. I will gather Lola, and you will be prepared to narrate a scandalous new tell-all."

* * *

With a slice of chocolate cake and a cup of tea, I give my confession, but I don't ask for absolution.

I don't ask for anything, because right now, I'm still basking in the afterglow.

My friends, however, clearly want something.

"Well, what do you think?" I ask when I finish.

Lola fans a hand in front of her face. "I think I need to see who's available tonight in my little black book. I might need to reenact your sex life."

"Come to think of it, maybe I should hire you to write a hot new line of naughty books," Amy says, but quickly she clears her throat. "But, Peyton . . ."

Those two words hang heavily in the air, signaling *advice to come*. Warnings I don't want to hear or heed.

"Guys, I'm fine," I say, cutting off her words to the wise before they arrive.

"I didn't even say anything yet," Amy says, holding up her hands in surrender.

"Listen, my mother already warned me. Be careful and all that. I am careful, I swear. I promise," I say, practically pleading with them to see this my way—the *have my cake and eat it too* way. "I just . . . want this. I know we can manage this. We made a plan. We'll finish out the tests and return to friendship. We did this before. Don't you remember?"

Lola furrows her brow, flinching. "You're not actually comparing a kiss at a college dance to sleeping with him?"

"Yes. Yes, I am," I say, because I have to. I have to see this the same way. No, I *choose* to. "We returned to friendship. It was no problem at that time. We'll do it again."

"That was different," Lola says firmly. "That was one kiss. This is sex. And it sounds like it's not just sex for either one of you."

But that's where she's wrong.

It's. Just. Sex.

It has to be.

That evening, I run a bath, drop in a bath bomb, and strip. I gave him a key last night, so right on time, he raps on the open bathroom door, walks into the steamy room, and finds me covered in bubbles, ready for the next test.

TRISTAN

On Sunday morning, I swing by a farmer's market I like, pick up some goodies, and grab coffee with some of my friends in the business. When I'm done, I pop back home, make lunch for my brother, and proofread his English paper on themes in dystopian literature. He finishes, turns it in online, then tells me he's going to join me at the gym for an afternoon workout.

I flinch, surprised. Barrett's not a gym guy. But I don't ask. I'm just glad he wants to exercise. On the treadmill, he jogs and texts and makes Instagram videos. At least I think that's what he's doing. His thumb-speed belongs in record books.

On the way home, we chat about college apps. "Is NYU still your first choice?" I ask, since he changes his mind frequently.

"I think so. The science department is good, and so is the English department."

I smile. "You don't have to know what you want to major in."

"Good. Because every day it changes."

"And that's okay," I say as we turn onto Madison Avenue.

"I also like Williams College. And Rutgers," he says, although he doesn't sound too enthused about those options.

"But?"

He shrugs. "Dunno. Guess I just want to be in New York." He offers me a small smile, and in it I see what he's not saying—he wants to be closer to home, closer to his friends.

I clap him on the back. "I'd love to have you in New York. But wherever you want to go is good with me."

"Yeah?"

"Yeah, of course. I want you to be happy."

He shakes his head. "No, I mean, you'd want me in New York?"

I laugh, and it turns into a scoff. "Yeah, I would. Not only do I love you, but I like you too, you little punk."

He doesn't answer, just smiles, and that's answer enough.

When we pass Peyton's shop, which is closed on Sundays, my eyes drift briefly to the display. There's an emerald-green teddy, and I picture her in it, chatting about Amy's new project while she puts on her makeup before going out with the girls. Or in that dark-purple pair of pajama shorts, standing in my kitchen, drinking coffee and trying to convince me to install an archery range at the restaurant. And in that right there—the leopard-print bra—laid out on the bed, waiting for me, tonight, tomorrow night, every night.

I blink the visions away. They're too powerful, too potent for me to linger on.

I look across the street, a block ahead of us, where I find a couple of guys on ladders removing the banner in front of Harriet's store.

And that's an image she'll love.

The sale is over, and my first thought is I can't wait to tell her when I see her in a few more hours.

* * *

Barrett leaves first, taking off for play practice. A little later, I'm on my way to Peyton's, walking uptown, when Barrett texts me.

Barrett: Just gotta ask. You can read, right?

Tristan: Yes. You can speak without using sarcasm, right?

Barrett: Wrong. Back to my point, you're reading these blogs, right?

Tristan: The food ones? You know I'm a food blog

fanboy. Of course I read my favorites. Just a few minutes ago, I found an awe-inspiring recipe for a jalapeño-drenched burger in sriracha sauce. Want one later?

Barrett: Obviously I do. I want two. But I'm not talking about what you're drenching burgers in.

Tristan: Aren't you at play practice?

Barrett: Aren't you at love practice?

Tristan: It's a project to help a friend grow her business, and it's working. See? I'm a magnanimous soul, supporting her in all her endeavors.

Barrett: Wow. This is going to be harder than I thought. Do you really believe that?

Tristan: Hello? Play practice?

Barrett: It's called a break. I'm taking one, and I'm texting you.

Tristan: Then I'll take a break from the sarcasm as I walk to Peyton's. I always love hearing from you.

Barrett: Dude, now is not the time to go all bro love on me. What I'm trying to say is this—Henry James said, "To read between the lines was easier than to follow the text." You need to read between the lines of her blog.

Tristan: You're quoting Henry James to me? Your education is worthwhile. God bless lit criticism classes in high school.

Barrett: Your sarcasm break was record-shatteringly short. Also, you are dodging the point.

Tristan: Listen, I get what you're trying to do, and I appreciate it. But you know what happens when you read between the lines? You make something bigger than it is.

Barrett: This isn't bigger than it is. This is exactly as big as it is. Time's up. Back to painting sets. By the way, in my paper, did you notice how dystopian futures are terrifying? And you don't have to read between the lines to know the hidden message is to live NOW.

I tuck the phone away as I reach Peyton's building. I'm sure he's right about dystopian futures, but that's not the world we're living in. This isn't *The Hunger Games*, and I don't need a bow and arrow to get out alive.

All I need are wits and a healthy sense of reality. I have both.

Reading between the lines would be as risky as volunteering as tribute. Besides, Peyton isn't sending me hidden messages in her blog. She's not writing me anonymous love letters.

The blog is a marketing vehicle for her store.

I should know, because it was my fucking idea for her to restart it. *To help her store.*

All that stuff she writes in it about wanting and craving and *feeling as good as she felt last night*—that exists in black and white to drive green.

Nothing wrong with that.

She loves that store madly. Cherishes her grandmother's legacy. Wants to protect it. *The Lingerie Devotee* is a means to a business end, that's all.

I would have to have an ego the size of Casanova's to think anything else of the tales she tells of late nights with lingerie and me.

Besides, the woman herself set the rules of engagement when she asked me to be her crash test dummy—*I need someone I can practice ripping a shirt off of who'll also rip off my panties.*

That was it. That was all.

She needed a willing participant, someone she trusts.

She's doing this because of that discount store anyway.

And with the discount over, the project will end

soon too. Not to mention that she only needs five scenes for Amy.

Best to enjoy tonight for what it is.

When I reach her place, I laser in on what matters now.

Figuring out how the hell all those couples in books are banging in the bath.

* * *

Candles flicker on the vanity. Soft music plays from her phone. Steam rises above the tub as she smiles softly from the water. The tiles are cool under my bare feet, but my body temperature is hot, hot, hot from her red hair, slicked back and wet, and the bubbles obscuring her breasts and belly. Her knees poke up.

"Hi," she says, and the sound is sweet, inviting.

"Hey," I say, drinking in the sight in front of me—this woman waiting for me in the tub.

Never in my dirty dreams did I imagine I'd walk in on this.

Maybe because tub sex was never on my fantasy list.

But it's on my reality agenda, and I'm so damn glad. Grabbing the bottom of my shirt, I tug it over my head.

"Look at you. Getting down to business," she says.

"Did you want me to do a long, drawn-out strip-tease? Wait. Don't answer that."

Her tongue lolls out, and she pants like a dog. "Striptease. Yes, please."

I shake my head, amused, as I unbutton my jeans. "Hate to break it to you, Gingersnap, but even if you have *Chippendales reenactment* on your list, I won't be doing it."

She pouts. "Really? Because I was going to add that. Are you sure?"

I'm not a dirty dancer. I definitely don't have the moves or the interest in doing a lap dance.

But when she puts it like that—I'm not sure I'd say no. If she asked me, I'd probably say yes. Fact is, I'd say yes to just about anything for her, only I can't let on how easy I am.

I shift the conversation. "Maybe I do need kneepads for this one," I say, tipping my forehead to the tub.

She narrows her brow. "Um, do you think you're going to be on top of me in the tub?"

As my jeans hit the tiles, my mind assembles the graphic novelization of this scene—in one panel, she's in the throes of ecstasy. In another, her mouth forms an O in pleasure. In the next one, she's coming.

Hmm. Seems that's as far as I've drawn—the endgame, over and over. I didn't consider the position we'd be in to get there.

"Because that won't work," she adds, gesturing to the tub. "Think about it. Are you just going to bang me while my body is underwater? My head would slam against the back of the tub. Ouch."

I kick off the jeans, shed my boxer briefs, and take over the pregame report. "No, Peyton," I say, walking over to her. "You're going to ride me. And you're going to ride me so fucking hard and so fucking good that neither one of us will care how much water we spill over the tub." Gripping my cock, I run my fist down its length, savoring the wild look in her blue eyes. Her lips part, and she seems to take a shuddering breath as she stares at my dick, transfixed.

I'd like to say this turning of the tables helps me stay in control of my runaway heart. As if taking the upper hand in our sex play somehow restores my power.

But it only makes me want her more, since she's staring at me like I'm all she wants too.

Then she rises like Aphrodite from the sea, red hair, naked body, beautiful and luminous.

And for tonight, she's all mine.

"Come on in. The water's nice."

I settle into the water, and she scoots around, squeezing in next to me, her bare flesh squeaking loudly against the tub.

I laugh.

She chuckles too.

Somehow she wedges herself into my side, but half her body is above the water now.

She frowns. "This is cozy."

But it doesn't sound like *cozy* is good. "And that's a strike against tub sex."

"Call me crazy, but I feel like my tub was designed for one person," she says, crushing her body closer as she tries to slink under the water more.

I adjust, making as much room for her as I can, but at six feet and two hundred pounds, I can't exactly suction myself into a smaller size. "I think most tubs were meant for one, but we're doing this. We're not backing down," I say, playing the hard-assed personal trainer who won't take no on the final crunch.

She stares sharply at me. "Did I say I was backing down?"

"Seems like it, since you're trying to lie next to me. Get on me, woman," I say, reaching for her waist and pulling her on top.

Her eyes widen as I position her, helping her straddle me in the tiny space.

Her knees slip, and she falls forward, collapsing on my chest. She laughs, pushing up.

"Kind of a dork, aren't you?" I tease.

"You try this. See if you can do it."

"I *am* trying this. And I want this. But I need you to want this too. I need you so damn slippery and wet that you don't care about anything else but fucking me hard."

She gasps, her shoulders shaking.

There. I'll keep her in the moment.

I reach for her face, clasp her cheeks, and pull her to me, sealing my lips to hers.

My plan, such as it is, is to kiss her soft, slow, and tender. Ease her into this position. Let her melt into a kiss so she can settle in this tiny space. But with her naked and wet on top of me, my best-laid plans fly the coop.

Curling a hand around her head, I haul her in for a fierce, possessive kiss. I kiss her deeply, my lips owning hers, my tongue exploring her sweetness.

She sinks into the kiss, all passion and surrender.

My brain goes hazy, and I'm sizzling everywhere in seconds. The kissing, the contact, the music, the water, the scents.

Dear God, the intoxicating candy-sweet scent of violet, or whatever the bubbles are. Everything goes to my head, and I can't slow down. I can't hold back.

That kiss in college had nothing on this kiss. This kiss blots out every other kiss in the history of the world as I consume her mouth, putting all my heart, all my body, into this moment.

She moves on me, sliding her pelvis down to mine, kissing me back the whole time.

Kissing me the way I want to be kissed.

By her.

Because hers are the only kisses I want. Fevered and passionate and full of so much . . . *emotion?*

I end that train of thought, fight desperately to stop assigning meaning that isn't there.

This kiss *can't* be full of emotion.

It can't be anything but sex and heat and an agenda.

I give in to that and only that—to the exploration of bathtub sex as an experiment. My hands glide down her body to her soft, supple ass, raising her up, guiding her over me.

She breaks the kiss, her palms on my pecs. "Tristan?"

"Yes?" I ask, as hope balloons inappropriately in me.

"My knees hurt," she says, whispering it like a confession.

"Do you want to get out?" I ask.

"No. I want to try. I really do want to try."

"Let me make sure you're ready." I slide my hand between her legs, groaning when I feel how slick she is there. "Gingersnap," I murmur.

"Fred," she purrs, somehow making that name sound sexy.

She lifts her hips, the water sloshing around as she gives me access to the paradise between her thighs. My fingers slide up and down, stroking her, touching her.

She shudders, letting her head fall back, looking more sensual than Aphrodite herself.

"I'm ready. I'm so ready," she says on a breathless pant.

Lust barrels through my body as I grip her hips and line her up. Water splashes along my stomach, and it ripples across her thighs, slapping over the tub. Glancing at the floor, I laugh. "We're going to need lots of towels."

But for now, I need to get her on me. Once more, I help her find a good position, and she rubs the head of my cock against her heat. My eyes squeeze shut as pleasure takes over momentarily, the incomprehensible sensation of this woman touching me.

Knowing me.

Having me.

I open my eyes as she widens her legs so she can sink down. But she winces.

"What's wrong?"

She shakes her head. "Nothing. Let's do this."

But she flinches again as she makes a second try.

I splay a hand on her belly, stopping her. "What is it?"

"This position . . ." she says with a sigh. "I'm sorry, but my toes are cramping, and my knees are killing me, and there's so much water, and the bubbles are . . ."

She lowers her face.

I tuck a finger under her chin, raising her face. "The bubbles are what?"

"Kind of stinging," she whispers. "Now that I'm getting all turned on and my legs are spread—and oh my God, I can't believe I'm saying this—there are soap bubbles in me, and it hurts."

I fucking love that she's saying it.

Her honesty is such a turn-on, and I don't mean physically. Her confession makes my heart trip.

Carefully, I settle my hands on her waist, helping her stand. I join her, then help her step out of the tub. "So bathtub sex is a no-go," I say, grabbing a towel and wrapping it around her.

"I like baths, but I think I like them solo."

I rub the towel over her hair. "I bet you'd love lounging in a tub and being fed chocolate."

Her eyes light up like sparklers. "Yes, let's do that next time. I'll take a long, luxurious bath, and you can join me. *Outside the tub.* Breaking off pieces of a chocolate bar."

Next time.

Those words echo.

The images flip before my eyes.

I want that next time more than I want this time.

But this time is all I have. I can't let myself forget that.

"Let's shower," I say, and we head into the shower, rinsing off the evidence of our botched experiment.

But it doesn't entirely seem like we failed.

As we joke about the perils and pitfalls of bathtub sex, it seems like we've discovered something new.

That failing together in bed can be as fun as succeeding.

Or maybe more fun, because it gives us another chance.

When we dry off, she slips into a soft light-blue robe that ends at her thighs, then tells me she's ready to try one last item. "Amy didn't ask me to test this one. When we planned the experiment, we toyed with testing how long till staircase sex kills your back, or how soon till rug burn kicks in if you do it doggie-style on a carpeted floor."

Damn. I'd like to fail and succeed at all of those with her. "But we're not doing any of those, I take it?"

She shakes her head, her eyes sparkling. "No. I read ahead. There's something else in the book that I want to try out. It's something I've never experienced before."

My heart slams against my chest in anticipation. "Whatever it is, I'll do it."

When she tells me, her scenario sounds like the best and worst way to end this brief no-strings-attached research project.

After all, this is my last chance with her.

All that's left for me to do is make it clear I'm 100 percent good with us returning to just being friends.

Like she wanted.

Like we said we'd do last night.

Is it a myth? An urban legend? Or the equivalent of a solar eclipse? Possible, but only once every few years.

Settling into the swath of purple and silver pillows on my bed, I straighten my spine, clear my throat, and adopt my best narrator's voice as I dive into the scene from Amy's book.

"As he spread my legs over his face, I drew him in deeper, letting him fill my throat. He thrusted up into me, and I nearly choked, but I was a determined chick-adee—determined to finish him any . . . freaking . . . second. Because I was close, so close. And once I tipped over the edge, I'd lose my mind with pleasure. His dick would fall from my mouth as I screamed my orgasmic praise to the heavens."

I stop, the temperature in my core shooting to the stratosphere.

Tristan's lips curve into a satisfied grin. He's

lounging next to me, propped on his side, his cock at full mast again.

I glance at the evidence that he's digging the story. "Guess this is getting you going?"

He shrugs impishly. "Maybe a little." He drags his fingers down my bare thigh. "And you? Is this better than soap and bubbles?"

"Yes. I'm feeling a little, how shall we say, squirmy? And yes, I know *squirmy* is not a sexy word."

His fingers roam to my knee. "On you it is."

"Is that so?"

He nods, bending his neck, pressing a kiss to my leg. "Everything is sexy on you. Now keep reading."

I return to the document on my phone.

"Focus, I told myself. Focus on the suction—"

But I can't concentrate because Tristan's lips flutter over my thighs, his scruff rubbing against my skin as he unties the ribbon on my robe. "Keep going," he murmurs.

I gasp as I try to read more.

"One long, deep suck. He groaned his appreciation for my efforts, but . . ."

He licks a line up my inner thigh, his soft tongue sending a spark of pleasure rushing through me. Screw the story. I toss the phone aside. He looks up from between my legs. "That's all?"

"Pretty sure I picked up the gist of the scene," I say, dragging my nails through his hair. I love the feel of his hair, his muscles, his skin. Love the contact, the connection.

So damn much.

"Think you can reenact it?" he asks.

"Yes," I say, already a little breathless from his touch and from anticipation. I want to taste him, feel him in my mouth, learn his flavors.

And I want to do it now, because if I stay in bed with him any longer, I will lose my heart to him. I already gave a little more of that organ to him in the tub just by telling him all the nitty-gritty details of why it wasn't working.

I've never been *that* open with a man. I've never felt that free.

And it felt tremendous.

Like I'd crossed a border and entered a country full of brand-new possibilities.

But we've reached the final scene, and this is my last chance to try out a certain kind of sexual intimacy. Admittedly I'm wary. I've never been a big fan of sixty-nine. It requires too much concentration and coordination. Too much mental work.

But as Tristan tugs my center toward his face, my mind takes a vacation. My body reports for duty. He spreads my legs and licks me.

I arch into him instantly, electrified from the first touch.

"Oh God," I cry out.

He groans against me, pressing a hot kiss to my core.

A bolt of heat radiates through me, and I part my legs wider, craving more of him. He groans against me, wrapping his hands under my ass and kissing me, devouring me.

I never knew what I was missing. Never knew till he touched me like this, but now I'm certain—no one has ever gone down on me like this before, not with this type of hunger.

"But in the scene . . ." I try to speak, because this isn't how they do it. And the test. We need to try the test . . .

He nods against me. "Um-hum."

"They do it at the same . . ." His tongue flicks against my clit, and my voice hits a new octave.

"Yep," he murmurs, lapping me up.

Threading my hands through his hair, I gaze shamelessly at the man between my legs. His gorgeous face. His passion. He's consuming me like I'm his last meal, and I want him to lick the plate clean and order seconds and thirds.

But that won't do. I can't linger in my own hedonism. I need to focus on the project and finish what I started.

For work, for the store, for my friend.

And most of all, for myself.

To put myself out there.

"Sixty-nine," I pant. "We need to try it. The scene. Need to see. If. We can. Come at the same time."

In a flash, he rolls to his back, pats his chest, and issues a command. "Drape those sexy legs over my face and take my cock deep in your mouth. Give it to me good, and I'll do the same to you."

I shiver at his filthy words, trembling with lust as I shed the robe and cover his body with my own. Wrapping my hand around the base of his hard cock, I kiss the head, flicking my tongue across him.

He jolts, cursing. "Holy fuck."

I laugh. "Yes, this feels religious for me too. I could worship your dick."

His groan is the sexiest sound I've ever heard. "I'm in heaven, Peyton," he says, but it doesn't sound dirty. It sounds reverent, and I'm sure heaven is where I am right now too, as he pulls me back to his mouth, licking me like I'm the best thing he's ever tasted. I suck him the same way.

Because he is.

He tastes spectacular. Clean but manly at the same time. I swirl my tongue over the head, then draw him in, loving the way he jerks his body up almost involuntarily as I move my lips along his delicious shaft.

We're not even listening to music this time, but I swear I can hear a symphony, picking up tempo, building to that rising crescendo toward the end when all the instruments come together at once, playing, soaring.

I lavish love on his cock, and he worships me with his mouth.

And the thought flashes clear and bright—we are acting out my command from last night. *Fuck me tonight, worship me tomorrow.*

Because this is worship.

This is a new kind of adoration, this intimacy.

I adore this man so much. I cherish him immensely. And I want to show him with my mouth and my tongue and my hands how very much he means to me. I want him to know that he's the man I trust.

But that's a little tough because he's going down on me like there's no tomorrow, and I'm losing my mind with pleasure. I can't concentrate. I can't focus. I can only feel.

I shudder as his tongue strokes faster, flicking my clit, driving me toward the edge.

And this is what I feel: *he's the one.*

He's the one who makes me feel so damn good, body and soul.

And heart.

Dear God, my heart beats loudly, insistently, because it's a part of tonight too.

Heart and hope and intimacy and hot, dirty dreams collide as my body tightens, pleasure coiling in me, my mind blurring.

I'm hot, so hot. Sensation grips me everywhere. Pleasure climbs up my legs in pulses.

I want to cry out. I want to moan, to groan, to say his name.

But I don't, because I want this moment more.

Not for the experiment.

I want it for me.

I want to know what it's like to feel *this* close to someone.

So close we crest the cliff at the same damn time.

Because I'm there, breaking and coming and tumbling into ecstasy.

I don't want to fall alone. I want his pleasure too. I'm desperately seeking it, and seconds later, it finds me as he fills my throat with his release.

He's salty and delicious, and I swallow him, savoring the taste.

Because it's him. Because I want him. Because I love him.

* * *

I play with the words in the back of my mind. *I'm falling in love with you.*

And more, so much more.

I want to go to your brother's homecoming as your date.

I want to walk into your bar and have everyone know I'm yours.

I want to see if staircase sex hurts my back, and if rug burn from doing it on the carpet is a real thing, and I want to have sex mishaps and sexual successes with you, only you.

And I want to kiss you goodbye in the morning someday. Someday soon. Maybe even tomorrow. Won't you stay with me?

The words are fighting their way to the shore, against the tide. They're eager to make landfall.

Even though that's not our deal.

This *is* our deal. This postcoital tangling of limbs,

as he pulls me close, wraps his arms around me, and kisses my cheek. "That's going out on a high note, I'd say. Do you agree?"

Going out on a high note.

That's where we're going. *Out.* We are unwinding. The hands on the clock are ticking back to friendship, minute by slipping-away minute.

But as each second passes, I desperately want to say something more. How do I get there though?

I slap on a smile for the time being. "Definitely. *Simultaneous orgasms are real, and you should definitely try it at home.* That's what I'll say in my blog." I haven't mentioned my blog to him in days. Is he still reading it? Has he picked up on what my mom claims she sees? Maybe this is how I can find out where he's at. "Hey, have you read the blog the last few days?"

He looks away, then back at me. "Yes."

It comes out a little guilty, like he's been caught spying.

"What do you think?" My nerves clamp down, but I have to push through. Feeling him out on the blog is a safe way to see if the last few nights are a one-way street.

I doubt my feelings are as transparent to him as they are to my mother, or my friends. Tristan isn't the type of guy to read between the lines on his own, not like the women in my life do. That's why I need to guide him through, feel him out.

"What do I think about your posts?" he asks carefully, like he wants to make sure he's understood the question.

"Yes. The things I said. The things I wrote." I do my best to keep my cool, even as my heart pounds with worry.

He takes a breath, giving him time, it seems, to consider what to say. "I enjoy your blog, Peyton. I always have. I'm glad you started it again."

My shoulders sag a little. That's not exactly giving me confidence. But I need to soldier on. "And do you think I've been accurately reflecting the tests?"

He's quiet for several long seconds. I try to read his eyes. To find the unspoken meaning in how he holds my gaze. Finally, he answers in a voice that's honest and vulnerable. "Yes."

Yes.

The one word reverberates between us and all my hope comes rushing back like a fountain. He sees what I don't fully say. He *can* see the hidden truths.

I smile so wide it might hurt, but nothing could hurt if he feels the same way I do. "I'm so glad," I say, breathless.

He smiles too. "Me too. It's working, right?" His tone shifts to a more professional one. "It's helped with business? All the things you've been saying about the experiments, the little details about how you want them to unfold. It's clearly doing the job because business is up, right?"

What?

Business? We're talking about business now? I thought we were talking about . . .

My heart sinks as awareness smacks me.

It was all in my head.

It was all in my heart.

He doesn't see what I see.

"It is," I say in my best keep-it-together tone as I share some of my numbers from the week.

My reality tilts once more. We are talking about business. Not the other things I've said in the blog.

Not the words about wanting, about craving, about needing.

About being adored.

My muscles tighten. My throat clenches. For a few horrifying seconds, I fear I might break into tears in front of him, but I swallow them down.

This sharp ache in my chest is necessary. This knowledge is everything I need to move past our experiment.

He's been reading my blog, and he sees it *only* as an experiment. *Only* as marketing.

He's not connecting to the hidden confessions I hardly realized were there.

He's only responding to the bigger purpose—the competitive one.

And that means when the clock strikes midnight, we return to friendship land.

At least we can return intact.

I haven't blurted out the truth of my heart, so I'm safe, and we're safe, and we'll return to who we were.

"So, there you go. It's a damn good thing I started it, and I'll just have to keep writing more about lingerie," I say in a cheery tone, trying to keep the mood featherlight to convince him the posts were only ever about the underwear.

Not about me.

Not about him.

"You should keep writing it, since you seem to enjoy it." He props his head in his hand. "Hey. I have good news. Did you know the Harriet's sale is over?"

"It is?" I ask, brightening.

"I saw it today. I couldn't wait to tell you. But then I got distracted by this beauty in the tub," he says, rough and raspy again, his eyes hooking into mine.

And the look in them is like a sign I should try one more time.

Because he looks at me like he feels the same way.

Put yourself out there.

"So you find me distracting?" I ask leadingly.

"You are highly distracting, Peyton."

That's promising, but then again, sex has been known to distract men. "What did you think of our tests? Did you learn anything?" I ask, trying to mask the hope in my voice.

He swallows and nods, his hazel eyes flickering with something darker, deeper.

That.

I want to know what *that* is.

That look is what I feel.

"What did you learn?" I ask, holding my breath,

hoping he's going to say he learned that I'm the one. Maybe he doesn't need to read between the lines of my blog to take a chance with me. Maybe he'll take it anyway.

His lips twitch in a wry grin. "That life doesn't always play out like a romance novel," he says, and my heart plummets.

I want the romance of the romance novel.

I want the sex and the love and the happiness.

"But what if it could?" I ask, pushing past the ache in my chest.

He taps my shoulder, grinning. "You didn't let me finish."

"Okay. Finish," I say, mentally crossing my fingers.

His fingers trace lingering lines on my hip as he says, "Life doesn't always play out like a novel, or even often. But sometimes, every now and then, you're so in sync with each other, you come together." He stops abruptly, like he was about to say something more, and I wait, on the edge of possibility. But all he says is "Right?"

There it is.

We are just sex.

He's not catching feelings for me.

I should kick him out. I should let him go. But I want one more time.

And he's going to give it to me.

"Right," I answer as I reach for him and bring him close, and he follows my lead.

Taking my wrists, he pins them over my head,

groaning with appreciation at the sight of me stretched out for him.

He doesn't say, *One last time*. He doesn't have to. It's clear.

What's clear, too, as he enters me is that getting over him now will take infinitely longer than last time.

And honestly, I'm not sure I ever did.

I think a part of my heart has always belonged to him.

Maybe that makes me dishonest.

Or maybe I'm finally being fully honest with myself.

As Tristan moves in me, breathing with me, moaning with me, I'm certain now. I gave a part of myself to him ten years ago. And I never took it back.

Trouble is, if I don't retrieve it now, I'll be lost for good.

* * *

When he leaves, he kisses me goodbye at the door, soft, sweet, and quick.

"Bye, Peyton."

"Bye, Tristan."

It feels like goodbye forever.

And I hate this feeling.

He holds the door open longer than he has to, then turns around and whispers my name. "Peyton?"

It sounds like the opening of a prayer.

"Yes?"

"What I meant to say is . . ." His lips part, but no more words come. He just looks at me like he's trying to understand the secrets of the universe. "What I meant to say is thank you."

It's like a hand grips my throat. "For what?" I choke out.

"For asking me to help you. For trusting me. I was so glad when you asked me. I didn't want it to be some other guy. I hate the thought of anyone hurting you ever again."

But you're hurting me right now. You're hurting me, and you don't even know it, you wonderful, beautiful, thoughtful man who doesn't love me the same way.

"You would never hurt me," I whisper.

He nods, swallowing roughly, his jaw tight. "I never would."

He steps into the hall, turns around one more time, and gives me a look that would make movie audiences throw their popcorn at the hero.

A look that would make them shout, "Kiss her, tell her, love her!"

But life isn't like the movies. It's not like the books.

That's what I learned this last week.

After the door shuts, I let the tears rain down.

TRISTAN

My hand doesn't move. It's stuck to her door like I can feel her through it. Like I can impart all the things I didn't say.

All the desperate, pathetic words that threatened to fall from my lips.

Like *I love you so much it hurts.*

Like *I don't want to read too deeply into your blog, but if you tell me you feel one-tenth of what I feel, I will be the happiest guy in the world.*

And like this—*By "come together," I didn't mean sex. It's hard for me to say what I mean because I don't want to lose you. I don't want to lose another person I love. But let me try to say it better. Let me rephrase. Life doesn't always play out like a novel, or even often. But sometimes, every now and then, you're so in sync, you come together like it was meant to be for the two of you. Right?*

And she'd say yes, and she'd throw her arms around

me and smother me in kisses, because this is our time. It has to be our time. We won't get another chance.

I've already let two opportunities pass me by.

I'd be an idiot to let the third one go.

Barrett would tell me as much. I smile privately, thinking of my brother. Of how I've tried to goad him into asking out Rachel, and how he's tried to push me into speaking the truth to Peyton.

How can I raise him to be a man of action, a man of truth, if I can't do it myself?

I can't say one thing to him and do another. That's not what my parents taught me, and it's not what I want to impart to Barrett.

In baseball, you get three strikes. You don't fucking walk away from the plate after two shots. You either try to whack the ball over the fence or you go down swinging.

I step away from the door then pace the hall, practicing, trying to figure out what the hell to say.

I'm going to do this, and I'm going to do it right.

And there's one way to do just that.

I need to go big. I need flowers and chocolate. I need to give her everything she wants.

It's Sunday night, but this is New York, a city that never sleeps, and I'm going to get the biggest bouquet and the best chocolate, and I'm going to come back and knock on the door and tell her the real reason I'm glad she asked me to be her partner.

Because I want to be the only one for her.

Always.

That's it.

Fueled by this plan, I head for the elevator, willing it to whisk me downstairs faster so I can canvas all the nearby shops, find everything she likes, and return like the heroes in books do.

Because even though I don't read those stories, I know enough. You don't show up empty-handed to tell the love of your life that you adore her.

You go big or you go home.

I rush down the street past a pair of late-night joggers, then a delivery truck dropping off a package. I race past a doorman in a fancy building, turning the corner toward the nearest bodega that sells flowers.

My phone buzzes.

Maybe it's her.

I slow slightly, grabbing it, and there's a message from Barrett.

Barrett: Fine. If it's going to come down to this, I'll be the bigger man. I'll go first. I finally told Rachel how I feel.

My grin stretches for a city block. Look at us, the Alexander men getting their acts together. I stop outside the store and reply.

Tristan: And how did it go?

Barrett: I actually told her a few days ago.

Tristan: Oh, you did? And that's good?

Barrett: It's good, but it's not what you think. I'm home. Want to talk?

And that's when I know tonight's confession has to wait.

PEYTON

The Lingerie Devotee: Don't Even Attempt to Try This at Home
Blog entry

Bathtub sex is a lie. Take a bath, have your lover feed you chocolate from beside the tub, then slip into a cute cotton robe and go to bed.

Or better yet, come into my store first. I'm having a sale on cute cotton robes, lace V teddies, and red bras and panties. Half off.

The Lingerie Devotee
Find me at You Look Pretty Today on Madison Avenue

TRISTAN

Barrett waits for me in the kitchen, drinking a can of LaCroix and scrolling through his phone.

"Hey. How was rehearsal?"

"It was good," he says, setting down his phone. He yanks open the fridge, grabs a can, and slides it to me.

"I'm not thirsty."

"Take it. You're going to need a drink. I'd give you a beer, but you don't keep liquor in the house."

I take the can, pointing it at him. "You're right. I don't keep liquor here, and I hope you don't drink till you're legal—"

"Yeah, yeah, yeah." He slides into a passable imitation of me. "*But if I do, call you, and you'll help me or my friends. And call an Uber*. I know. But this isn't about drinking. This is about something else."

I frown, cracking open the can of raspberry-flavored water, the back of my neck prickling. I have no clue what he needs to talk about, but I'm imagining the worst—drugs, depression, a friend committed suicide. I'm not the praying type, but I offer a silent request anyway as I take a drink then set down the can. "So, evidently we need drinks to talk?"

"It's metaphorical." He chugs back some of his beverage, puts down the can, then exhales. "My liquid courage."

I squeeze his shoulder, worry thrumming through me. "What's going on?" I ask evenly, because I don't want to let on that he's freaking me out. "Tell me what happened."

He drags a hand through his hair and breathes in loudly through his nostrils. "So . . . I took your advice. I told Rachel how I feel . . ."

"And?" Every muscle in my body tenses.

"And she agreed that I should go for it with Eli." The words come out so quickly I'm not sure I heard him correctly.

"Come again?"

"Eli. He's on the tech crew too. He's into robotics and has shitty taste in music, since he likes pop, but I can forgive that because he has a wicked sense of humor. Also, he's a Yankees fan."

If I thought he shined when he talked about Rachel, that had nothing on the sweetness I hear in his voice now. And with that, the dots start to connect. "When you were saying you wanted to tell Rachel how you feel, and that you needed to do it in your own time, you meant she was the first person you told that you like Eli?"

"Yeah. She wasn't surprised. And don't worry— she's not heartbroken. She didn't think of me that way, and I'm glad. You, however, seem surprised." His voice is strained, and there's a touch of fear in his eyes.

And I don't want him to be scared. Not for one second.

He's brave.

He's completely brave. My seventeen-year-old brother just came out.

"Yes, I'm surprised. But it doesn't matter." I laugh, relieved that he's telling me he likes dudes rather than that someone broke his heart, or he's addicted to opiates, or he's unhappy every second of the day. "I was worried she'd hurt you, or that you were going to tell me you were depressed, or a million other things. But you're not." I let out a huge breath as I smile like a proud dad. "You're telling me what you like, and I think that's awesome."

He narrows his eyes, but the sliver of a smile appears. "It is?"

"Yes! God, yes. You know yourself. You understand yourself. That is fantastic. *This* is fantastic."

He lets out a huge sigh, like he's been taking on the weight of the world. "I was really worried."

"Why? Why would you worry?"

"Because you're *soooo* into girls."

My smile takes over. "And that means I'd want you to be *soooo* into girls?"

His eyes widen. "Um. Yeah. You've been pushing me to ask out Rachel for, like, forever."

"You've been acting like you liked her! You spend all this time with her, and you're all happy and upbeat when she's around, and you pretty much said you were going to ask her out. We made a bet. Why would I think anything else?"

"Fine. I led you on, but I just thought you wanted me to be like you. All manly and bearded and totally into curves."

A laugh bursts from deep inside me. "News flash. Whether you're gay or straight isn't what makes you manly."

He seems to consider this for longer than I would have expected, his hazel eyes darkening, turning serious. "What does, then?"

His question is completely earnest.

And it's why I come home every night. It's why I show up for him. So he has someone to ask these questions. Someone who can answer.

But even though I was dead wrong about who he likes, I know I'm dead right when I give him my answer. I clasp his shoulder. "What makes a man a man is when he owns up to his mistakes, when he acts with integrity, when he speaks with honesty, and when he looks out for those he loves. And you . . ."

I shake a finger at him, my voice breaking for the first time since my mom died. "I love you, Barrett. I love you like crazy, and I'm sorry if I made you think you had to like girls. You can like girls, or girls and boys, or just boys. Or everyone. Love is love, and I want you to love whoever you want. Okay?"

His eyes shine, and he nods several times, pursing his lips like he's holding back emotion too. I draw him in for an embrace, a long big-brother bear hug that I don't want to break.

But I do because I have to know something. I poke his chest. "Did you ask Eli to homecoming?"

Barrett smiles. "I did."

"And?"

His answer comes in the form of a grin.

I grin too. "So, he said yes?"

"He did. You'll like him. He's cool."

"And he's smart, obviously, if he likes you." Sunshine fills my chest. This is good. This is so damn good.

Barrett blows on his fingernails then brushes them across his chest. "I am a prize."

"No doubt. You're an Alexander man. And I'm glad you have a friend like Rachel. Glad you have someone you could talk to. Even if you told her before me." I frown, giving him an over-the-top pout. "But you did trick me with your bet."

He raises one brow. "Did I though?"

"Didn't you? You said you'd ask her out."

He raises a finger to make a point. "I believe my deal was—if you ask out Peyton, I'll tell Rachel how I feel."

My jaw comes unhinged. "You sneaky little punk,"

I say in admiration. I flash back on all our recent Rachel conversations. Come to think of it, he never did say he'd ask her out. He always said he'd tell her how *he felt*. And he did tell her.

He beat me to it, even though it wasn't a contest.

My little brother manned up before I did. And he did something even harder—seeing himself truly, and being honest with himself, his friends, and his family.

He taps his toe. "And did you tell Peyton the truth?"

For the first time in years, maybe even since our mom was alive, I speak aloud about Peyton with absolute honesty.

"That I'm in love with her? That I fell in love with her in college? That I wanted to have a real chance with her a few years ago before Gage came back in her life? That she's the one I want to spend my nights and mornings with?"

He rolls his eyes. "Dude. You sound like you're in one of those chick flicks."

I laugh, loving that he ribs me still. "And what of it?"

"Save it for the woman. Tell her." He stabs a finger on the kitchen counter. "Tell her now. As a wise man once told me: 'I don't want you to wait too long and then regret it,'" he says, quoting me back to me. "Do you know what I mean?"

"I do. I absolutely do. And I was going to tell her tonight."

"Tell. Her. Now."

I nod dutifully, a good soldier.

I pick up my phone to call her, to see if I can swing by, but it goes straight to voicemail.

And that's where it stays when I call again that night—a few times—and when I wake in the morning.

30

PEYTON

Marley opens the door cautiously, glancing around like she might get in trouble. When she spots me behind the counter, she offers a toothy grin. "Hi."

Her voice is stretched thin, and I wonder if she did something wrong, or if I'm giving off don't-disturb-the-bear vibes.

Probably the latter.

My vibes are dipped, battered, and fried in misery today, and no one wants to be near me.

She reaches into her purse, fishes around for something, and extracts a Lulu's chocolate bar with coconut and caramel.

"I thought you might need this. You seem . . . not yourself," she says, taking tentative steps toward the counter and setting the bar down gently, like I might attack.

I smile faintly at the gesture. "I do need this. Thank

you." I grab the bar, rip open the wrapper, and bite into the corner, just as the bell tinkles.

Shit.

I can't eat chocolate at the register. I can't eat anything surrounded by all this silk and satin and lace.

I'm a piggy-pig-pig.

I shove the candy under the counter, checking my fingers to make sure I don't have evidence of my chocolate therapy on them.

"Was it good?"

I raise my face, relieved to see Daniella. "It was delicious," I admit.

"You okay?" she asks, striding over to the counter.

Marley steps in, smiling brightly. "She's great. I was just raving about this chocolate, and I brought her some and made her eat it, and it's all my fault."

I laugh, but I can't let her take the blame for my indiscretion, especially for something so innocuous and so clearly my responsibility—my sad, sour mood.

"Actually, I'm in a funk, and Marley is Wonder Woman, attempting to save the day by delivering my favorite thing."

Daniella smiles at both Marley and me. "I had a feeling you were in a funk. I read your blog."

I gulp. "Sorry. You must have caught it before I took it down earlier. I shouldn't have posted that."

She's not the first one to notice the blog. Amy called me this morning, and Lola did too. "Was that a cry for help?" Lola had asked.

"Because it sure seemed like one," Amy had seconded.

They'd proceeded to conduct an early morning therapy session that consisted of a lot of "chin ups" and "But are you sure that's what he meant?"

Yes, I was sure.

I'd raised the issue of *more* with Tristan. I'd tried to talk to him. I'd made it as clear as the blue sky above.

And what did he do?

He *thanked* me.

He motherfucking thanked me last night.

If that isn't a "he's just not that into you," I don't know what is. The man clearly wanted to bang me—*you're so pretty, I want you, blah blah blah blah blah*—but that was all he wanted.

Friendship and lingerie.

Nothing more.

That's why I didn't answer his missed calls this morning when I saw them wallpapering my phone. I didn't even listen to his voicemails. What's the point?

And you know what? It was all my fault. I can't even be mad at him because I asked him for this very thing—*be my tester, help me out, and oh, I'm hot for you, let's have a bang-a-thon.*

I set myself up to fail.

And now I have to suck down all these icky feelings and be the best damn bra saleswoman I can be. I wave a hand, dismissing my mood as if it's a dust mite, and I smile at Daniella, returning to her question. "I'm all good. It was a momentary funk."

Daniella narrows her eyes. "Was it?"

"Of course. Funk be gone. Enough about me, statistical goddess. Tell me how the math bra went," I say, zeroing in on her.

"It was great. I feel great. But I didn't come here to talk about lingerie. I came to talk about you."

I blink. "What about me?"

She sighs sympathetically. "I was worried about you. Because of your blog. It's not like you to post something like that. And I just wanted to make sure you were okay."

My heart squeezes at the gesture. The lovely gesture of a customer checking up on me. "I'm going to be fine."

"You really liked the guy, didn't you?"

A lump forms in my throat. "I did. Well, obviously I still do. The feelings didn't go away overnight. Wish they did."

"Why do you like him?"

I shake my head, not wanting to answer.

But she's persistent. "How *do you feel* with him?"

Marley pipes up. "She feels amazing."

I snap my gaze to my assistant, who's not normally so outspoken. "Why do you say that?"

"Well, you're always a good-natured person, but in the last week, you've come into the store with this spring in your step, a saucy secret in your eyes, and a grin you can't wipe off your face."

Damn. My cheery, go-getting assistant is an observational guru too. A traitorous smile twitches across my lips, but I wipe it off.

"Like that," Marley says, pointing. "You can't stop smiling. This guy, this project—he makes you happy."

Yes. Yes, he does. He makes me feel like the sun and the moon and the stars. He treats me like a goddess and looks at me like I'm a work of art.

"He does. He makes me incandescently happy." I sigh, full of the weight of unrequitedness. "But he doesn't want the same thing I want."

Daniella tilts her head. "Are you sure though?"

I nod, dejected. "I'm positive. And you know what? I have a whole store full of lace and silk to help me get over him." I rub my palms together. "Now, as for you, why don't you let me help you find another sexy little number that'll make you feel like a Botticelli?"

"If you insist."

"I do." I happily help her because I love what I do, and I welcome the distraction.

She chooses a stars and planets bra, and as I ring her up, I ask about her plans for the week.

"I am on the hunt for a fun new girls' night out activity. I'm in charge of planning it this time, and I have nothing so far," she says.

Fortunately, I have just the answer. "Try goat yoga. My girlfriends and I are going to do that. We took Cirque du Soleil classes too, and they were horrible but also fun."

"Those sound like a blast," she says, then narrows her eyes at me, serious again. "And I'm going to pop in next week to buy more little darlings and to check on you." She waves goodbye, then says in a hopeful tone, "But I have a feeling."

When the door shuts, I see a familiar silhouette walk past my store.

My ex. He's in a suit, hair slicked back, talking on the phone, heading uptown.

And I feel nothing.

I turn away from the window.

I don't care where Gage goes or walks or what he does. He's my past.

Even if he skirts near my present, I'm not bothered.

He's just another guy on the streets of New York.

He's not the one I want to see walking into my store, coming to my home.

My shoulders shudder as a wave of longing crashes over me.

"Hey." Marley's voice is soft but insistent, her hand gentle as she touches my arm. "Get some fresh air. You're sad, but you shouldn't be sad." Her soft brown eyes are wise beyond her years.

"Why do you say that?"

She shrugs happily. "Like Daniella said, I have a feeling. Go for a walk. See if you get a feeling too."

She shoos me out the door.

And as I walk along Madison Avenue, heading downtown, savoring the changing colors of fall, I reflect on their words. *I have a feeling.*

And my mom's. *You have a vibe.*

Lola's too. *I've seen the way you two are together.*

And then Tristan's, in bed, before the first time. *You have no idea.*

And all the other things, said and unsaid, that have passed between Tristan and me over the years.

Back in college. When we were friends. When we kissed. When we returned to being friends again.

And over the last nine months since I've been single. How he makes me the owner's special. And gives me chocolate. And listens to every word I say.

And the past few nights. The way he's touched me, looked at me, whispered my name.

I saw so much in his eyes. So much truth and honesty.

I was searching for confirmation in words. But maybe he already gave it to me in other ways. Or perhaps I wasn't seeing between the lines.

And maybe I need to find a way to give him more than a fishing expedition of effort. More than feel-him-out questions about my blog or the experiments or friends with bennies.

I need to tell him in no uncertain terms.

Because regrets are for haircuts and exes.

And I don't want Tristan to be an ex-anything.

I turn around.

31

TRISTAN

I'll give her till eleven to call me back.

That should be enough time for her to wake up, get dressed, go to work, settle in for the day, and listen to messages.

That's civilized—give the woman a little time and space to deal with her business.

I go into work early, checking her blog on the way. But there's no new post, and my heart sinks a little lower.

No worries though. She's probably busy with Monday morning work stuff. At the restaurant, I handle the usual smattering of phone calls from suppliers and emails regarding inventory.

When eleven rolls around, my phone is still bereft of messages or texts from her.

I open the call log, about to call her again, when the door swings open. Likely a customer coming in for an early lunch.

I do a double take when I see who it is.

My jaw ticks as Gage walks over to the counter, grabs a stool, and flashes me a grin.

"Hey, Tris. What's up? Saw a write-up for this spot in a food blog, so I'm meeting a client here for an early lunch." He extends a hand to shake, like we're buddies reconnecting after a long absence.

I don't take it. I slide him a menu. "Here you go."

"Whoa. What's with the cold shoulder?"

Is he for real? "Excuse me?"

Gage looks around. "Isn't this a place of business?"

"Yes," I say, clenching my fists. "And here's the way to do business. You look at the menu. You place an order. That's how it works."

Gage gives me a *c'mon, man* sigh, then flashes me a smile. "Look, Tris. I know you wanted Peyton long ago. You didn't get her. It happens. I don't have her either. Let's just move on." His eyes drift down to the menu, perusing the fare. "Now, what do I want to drink while I wait?"

I seethe.

This guy.

This fucking guy.

I park my hands on the bar, about as aggressive as I can be without being aggressive.

"Let me make something clear." He looks up from the menu, and I gesture from him to me. "You and I are not the same."

He tilts his head and arches a well-groomed brow. "But we kind of are. We both wanted her." He studies me, waiting for me to respond perhaps. I remain stone-faced and silent, and he laughs. He actually laughs. "Wait. Did you think I didn't know you were hot for her? I knew the whole time. I knew in college, and I knew the last few years." He scratches his jaw. "And I guess the whole world knows too, thanks to her ridiculous blog. Like I didn't know you were her trick pony," he scoffs.

Temper burns through me, raging like a forest fire. But I think of Barrett and what I told him last night. The measure of a man isn't fists, or fights, or who thumps his chest the hardest.

It's integrity. It's truth. I speak mine as I lean forward. "Her blog isn't ridiculous. And you know nothing about me, or her, or us. Also, we don't serve your kind around here." Snatching the menu from him, I point to the door. "No shirt, no shoes, no assholes. Get the hell out of my restaurant. You lost the best woman you'll ever have, and I would feel sorry if I could muster a single emotion for you, but I can't. So goodbye."

He holds up his hands in some sort of *excuse me* gesture. "You don't have her either."

"Once again, you're missing the point entirely." I take a beat and let go of my anger. "But then again, you always did."

He scoffs, pushes away, and walks out.

As he leaves, I picture the time he walked back into her life a few years ago. When I'd bought flowers and planned to ask her out.

Now I'm not in the least bit worried about that

chump. I don't need to beat him to her doorstep. He's not winning her back ever again.

But I'm also not wasting another minute waiting. I did that for ten years, and I'm done frittering away another nanosecond.

I tell my assistant manager I need to handle some errands, then I leave and head straight for her store.

When I reach it ten minutes later, she's rounding the block, a look of intense focus on her face, her lips parted, like she's practicing a speech.

I walk right up to her, stop in front of her, and clasp her cheeks.

She startles, then says, "*Oh.*"

I don't wait. I say everything I should have said last night. "I love you. I love you. I love you. Please love me too."

32

PEYTON

This is the real dream.

This is the moment that's so surreal, it might be my deepest fantasy. Powerful and potent and the one I want now.

The one I've only realized I had in the last few days. But it's been growing inside me for years. I've been watering the seed of it, tending to it, readying it to bloom.

Shivers run down my arms, and they're not from the slight chill in the air. They're from my reality.

The man I love holds my face, gazes deep into my eyes, and asks me to love him.

I slide my hands up his chest, touching him, needing to connect with him. "You don't have to ask. I'm already there. I love you," I say, at last speaking the words I tried to say twelve hours ago. "I should have told you last night. I wanted to tell you, but I was scared. I'm not scared now, and I was coming to find you and tell you too."

His lips curve in a grin. "But I found you."

"I always want you to find me."

"I always will." He sighs, and the sound that comes with it is rich with joy. "Kiss me," he tells me. "Kiss me like you love me."

"I can't kiss you any other way." I brush my lips to his, gasping at the feel of him.

In a way, it's our first kiss.

It's the first time we've touched this honestly, this truthfully. It's our first kiss knowing the score. And that's how we kiss, like we've been waiting years to fall in love fully, completely, with the right person.

He holds my face the whole time, like he doesn't want to let go of me.

I don't want him to either. I want to be in his arms, with this man I trust and love and cherish.

His lips travel over mine, an eager exploration as we enter this new land together.

Love.

Real love.

With true intimacy.

When we break the kiss days later—okay, maybe it's only a few minutes—he's smiling at me and I'm grinning at him.

"I should have done that years ago," he says, shaking his head.

"Same here."

He runs his thumb along my cheek. "I wanted to a

few years ago. Before . . ." He trails off, not saying his name. He doesn't need to.

"You did?"

He nods solemnly. "I was all ready to give you flowers and go to your house and ask you to go out with me. That cologne you gave me had me convinced."

I laugh, remembering that gift. "You did smell awfully yummy when you wore it."

"I was stupidly convinced the cologne was a sign."

"Maybe it was, and I didn't realize it. Maybe I wasn't prepared for real love then. But I am now, and I'm not letting you slip away." I grab the neckline of his shirt for emphasis, clutching him tight. "I'm not."

He gathers me close, kisses my hair, and whispers, "I won't let you. I promise. Besides, I have nowhere to go but to you, Peyton."

My throat hitches, but this time I don't try to swallow down the tears. They're tears of happiness, and I let them fall.

And I'm even happier when he kisses them away, his lips soft and tender on my cheek. "What do you say we conduct a new experiment?"

I pull back to meet his eyes. "And what's that?"

"How about we try love and sex and friendship? All of those wrapped up together?"

I tap my chin, like I'm deep in thought. "Hmm. Love, sex, and other shiny objects. I'm game."

That night after work, he comes over, and I pounce on him the second he walks through the door.

We kiss like lovers in love, and like friends in love too.

He carries me to my bed and strips me down to nothing. I am bare before him, heart and soul. "Tristan, it was never just sex for me."

He runs his fingers down my neck. "It was always love. Even when I fuck you, I'll always be making love to you."

I shudder, wild with anticipation as I take off all his clothes too.

When he's inside me, I let go with him in a whole new way.

This is everything I've ever wanted.

Real intimacy.

Real closeness.

Real love.

* * *

"Victory is mine! And the game goes to the fifty-five-year-old." My mom thrusts her racket in the air, showboat that she is.

I shake my head, but I'm smiling as I congratulate her on her win on the badminton court. "You're the champ, mom. But I do have a question for you. When you lie about your age, why do it by one year? Why not pretend you're, say, twenty-nine?"

She tuts, like that's the silliest notion. "Because then we'd be twins, sweetheart."

"Ah, well. That explains everything."

"Also," she says, as we exit the court after my epic pummeling, "I'm ready for my *I told you so*."

"Do you want me to serve it up with quinoa?"

"Excellent idea. Let's get a quinoa bowl and you can tell me all about what the vibe turned into."

We head to a café and I tell her the rest of the story. "And real love is awesome," I add, when I finish the tale. "Also, you were right about Tristan and me having a thing. Does that make you happy?"

"No. What makes me happy is that you chose wisely. And I don't simply mean the man. You chose boldness. That was brave. That was worth it, wasn't it?"

I nod, agreeing with my whole heart. "When it comes to love, being bold is so much better than being careful," I say, so glad I went for it with the man I adore.

"Keep being bold. Love is worth it."

"And on that front, once again, you're right."

As we dine on quinoa, I consider myself lucky to have so many amazing women in my life—women who've helped me reach for and realize so many dreams.

From Mimi, to my mom, to my best friends, to the women I encounter in my job, they've all played a part in where I am today.

And I'm exactly where I want to be.

33

TRISTAN

She doesn't stow away a small family under her dress.

That's good because her dress comes to just above her knees.

It's ruby red, and she looks like a jewel. The music shifts from some pop star to some other pop star, and I wrap an arm around her waist as we man the punch table.

"Are you wearing red lace under that?" I whisper, my voice already husky as I picture unzipping this dress later.

"Maybe," she says with a flirty, dirty look. "Or maybe I'm wearing green. To match the shirt I bought you." She tap-dances her fingers down the forest-green Henley. "Have I mentioned how good you look in this shirt?"

"Good enough to get me naked later so you can have your way with me?" I ask in a growl.

"That's exactly my plan."

"You should conduct an experiment to see how quickly you can take it off me. I'll do the same when it comes to stripping off your dress to see if you're wearing green." Around us, the seniors at Barrett's school dance, laugh, and snap pictures. "But I doubt it. You usually match your undies to your clothes."

She wiggles her eyebrows. "Very observant. Also, green is not my color when it comes to lingerie."

"Why not?"

"It makes me look like a leprechaun," she says, flicking her red hair.

I run a hand through those strands, tugging her close. "On you, Peyton, the leprechaun look is sexy."

She rolls her eyes as someone clears his throat.

We yank apart to find that *someone* is my brother.

"Don't you know the chaperones aren't supposed to make out?" he chides us.

He's not alone. The guy next to him with olive skin and green eyes shakes his head in amusement. "Adults today. You can't leave them alone, Bear."

Bear. Eli already has a nickname for my brother.

"Seriously. What does it take to get some punch around here?" Barrett asks.

"All you have to do is ask nicely. And not slurp," I say.

Peyton sticks a hand in the air and waves. "Hello? Introductions, gentlemen."

As I ladle some punch, I second her. "Yes, Barrett. Make the intros."

After I pour the beverages, we all shake hands and

say hello, and then Barrett and Eli head back to their crew, joining Rachel and the rest of them.

I turn to Peyton. "I suppose I should apologize for constantly putting my hands on you, but I can't seem to find it in me."

"I would never accept such an apology. Because *on me* is my favorite place for your hands." She smiles as the music shifts once again. The tune is instantly familiar.

She grins like she has a secret. *Our* secret. "I asked them to play this. I've always wanted to kiss you again to this song."

Cyndi Lauper's love song fills the gymnasium, and I take Peyton's hand and bring her to the dance floor.

And I give her what she wants.

It's what I want too.

And this time is our time.

For all time.

34

PEYTON

A few months later

The blog worked for my brother. He sent an ultrasound picture to the family chat the other day. A tiny little peanut that's growing in Holly.

Jay: Thought you might like this first shot of the newest Valencia.

Mom: The lingerie worked!

Jay: You told mom we bought lingerie from your shop?

Peyton: Obviously. Also, congratulations!!!!! Was it the leopard print that did the trick?

Jay: Yes, do you want us to name the baby Leopard Print Valencia?

Mom: That is a perfect name. Also, I'm so happy for you!

Peyton: And I hope you have a girl so I can buy her her first bra someday.

Jay: Can we please not talk about bras yet?

Peyton: Sure. But mark my words, if you have a girl, I will definitely be taking her underthings shopping. Count on it.

The blog worked for business too.

It's still working.

Case in point—a determined woman in a trench-coat who marches into my shop at the end of the day and declares in a posh tone, "I'm looking for a teddy that will make me want to rip off my lover's shirt."

"Are we talking all the buttons flying everywhere?"

She sweeps her arm out wide. "Ping, ping, ping. Literally everywhere."

"Let me show you a few items that I bet you'll love," I say, and guide the woman to our new collection of teddies.

"Yes. Gorgeous," she declares as she flicks through the display. "Oh yes. Delicious." She pauses, eyes lighting up. "Oh, my yes. Must have that. I better go try this on right now."

"Don't forget to try the new pink one too. You'll look pretty in pink," Marley says, chiming in.

"Good idea. Plus, it'll make me look innocent," the woman says with a wink.

"God bless pink for that and other reasons. I'll show you to the dressing rooms," Marley says.

A few minutes later, the woman emerges, all the lacy teddies draped on her arm. "I'll take them all. Including this pink one. I'll have something to wear for the shirt ripping, the panty ripping, the staircase routine, and then for whatever else I decide to add to the naughty mix."

I beam. "I like the way you think."

"And I suspect you'll love the way they make you feel every time you wear them," Marley says as she rings up the woman.

When the customer leaves You Look Pretty Today, I lock the door behind her, then give Marley a thumbs up. "Well done."

We close up, arranging displays and making sure the store looks fabulous to passersby in the night.

"That was a great day," Marley says as she straightens some pink bras. "Business just gets better and better."

"It sure does," I say. "And you've played a big part in that."

Marley is a kick-ass employee, so good at her job that I promoted her. She's funny as hell too, and we take turns blogging now, sharing our respective adventures in lingerie.

Tristan's original instinct was right—the blog and the social media that goes with it have played a huge part in keeping my shop competitive. We've been able to hold our own against Harriet's, and we're doing it in a way that would make Mimi proud—with personal service for all our customers, making sure they go home feeling beautiful in what they wear beneath the clothes they show the world.

Marley flashes a naughty little grin. "Well, I do happen to love lingerie as much as my boss does. So thank you for letting me write about it with you." She's a kindred spirit, and that's exactly who I enjoy spending my days with here at the store.

"There's no one I'd rather share a pen with," I say.

"And on that note, how about slipping me some of that new La Perla shipment? I have a hot date tonight," she says, wiggling her eyebrows.

"Ooh. I want details tomorrow. And yes, grab something lacy and lovely."

"I will, and this guy, I have a good feeling about this one."

"I can't wait to hear more."

And after work, I like spending my evenings with my girlfriends from time to time. They're my people too, and always will be, so after we close, I head to Gin Joint to catch up with Lola and Amy.

Amy's bouncing when I arrive, but she usually is. The woman has more energy than all the coffee beans in Columbia.

She's holding something behind her back, and when she brandishes it, I squeal.

Lola does too, and Lola is not a squealer. "Isn't it beautiful?" Lola says, going first.

I grab at the book, with its bright-yellow cover and red title. The illustrated couple on the front is perfectly cheeky and adorable.

"*Sex and Other Shiny Objects*," Amy declares, handing me my advance copy of the book I contributed to. Immediately, I flip to the back, checking out the "Do and Don't Try This at Home" guide that I penned for her.

I smile like a loon as I reread the blog posts—the posts that helped me realize I was in love with my best friend. "Ooh, I love this one especially." I adjust my stance, adopting my librarian pose, and I dive into the revised post I wrote about bathtub sex.

"Let's talk about bathtub sex again. Yes, my pretties. It is a lie. Your knees hurt, your toes cramp, and your lady parts just might sting for hours. But what's not a lie is this—bathtub love. Have a soak with your lover. Snuggle together in a tub. Get close. Or better yet— luxuriate in bubbles and have a chat with him or her about your day. After, when you're all warm and relaxed, make your way to the bedroom. There, just go for the golden ticket. I'm talking the simultaneous prize. It's rare, and it's unlikely. But that's why it's all the more

fun. Make it a quest. Try it several times. Every night. I tried it with the man I love, and let me tell you—it's spectacular. But then, so is he."

A shiver runs through me as I remember that night. And, well, all the other nights we've chased after the elusive simultaneous finish of the sixty-nine. Some nights we catch it. Sometimes one of us flies first. But every time feels like the best time. Because I'm with him.

When I look up, they're both staring at me like I'm a goofball.

"You're so happy it's ridiculous, and I love it," Lola says.

"Yes. Yes, I am. Drinks are on me. Especially since business has been oh-so-good, thanks to this blog. Check this out," I say, as I click over to the comments section, showing them the exchange between Lovey Buns and Sweet ums.

Sweet ums: Thank you, Lingerie Devotee, for revealing the truth about bathtub sex. Like I tell my lovey buns, it's just not happening.

Lovey Buns: But I'm willing to try again. Practice makes perfect, as they say.

Sweet ums: Bathtub sex is not yoga. It is not a practice.

Lovey Buns: But yoga makes it possible to get into all sorts of positions. Including in the tub, sweet ums.

Sweet ums: No. Not in the tub, lovey buns.

Lovey Buns: Out of the tub then? Maybe when you're wearing that babydoll nightie?

Sweet ums: That is a pretty number. I do love how you indulge my lingerie habit.

Lovey Buns: And that habit, I will definitely keep practicing.

Sweet ums: And in that case, practice will make perfect.

I close the browser window as my friends nod approvingly at the couple's exchange. I'm pleased too that everything worked out as it was meant to be for Sweet Ums and Lovey Buns—they are perfect together.

We order a round of Devil's Teeth, and after we ooh and aah over the book cover again, Lola takes a deep breath, the signal that she's about to make an announcement. "So...are you ready to hear the latest about you know who?"

"Chris Hemsworth?" I toss out a random name.

"Scott Eastwood?" Amy pitches in.

"Tom Ellis?"

"That hot guy on that new Netflix show you love?"

Lola laughs, shaking her head at each suggestion. Then she draws a deep breath and answers in a foreboding tone. "Lucas."

"Um, yes," I deadpan. "I've been dying to hear the latest since you had to spend those 24 hours with him."

"A delicious 24 hours," Lola adds.

"A wild and naughty 24 hours," I chime in.

Amy stabs the table with her finger. "I demand a full report now, wild, naughty and delicious."

Lola straightens her spine. "Here's the latest with Lucas."

I sit, enrapt, as she tells us what's going on with the guy she had a thing for ten years ago, the guy who appeared in her life again a few days ago.

I'm all ears, because I can't wait to hear what happens next with Lola and the one who got away.

EPILOGUE

Tristan

Several Months Later

I blindfold her.

"Are you sure I can't see it?"

"I'm positive," I tell Peyton as I guide her to the back room of my bar. The cornhole board still claims center stage, but I've added shuffleboard too. And another item at her request.

Well, sort of.

I reach for the rubber hatchet I left on the ground.

I'm *not* letting her throw a metal one. I'm not letting *anyone* toss a metal one. But the woman has a thing for ax throwing, and I have a thing for making her dreams come true.

"Hold out your hands."

She stretches them in front of her, and I set the rubber ax in her palms.

"Is this what I think it is?" she asks with delight.

"Sort of." I move behind her and untie the blindfold, letting it fall to the floor.

Her smile fills the room when she sees the target I've installed. "It's ax throwing for my princess lumberjack."

She dances a little jig as she raises the toy ax made of hard, sharpened rubber over her shoulder and takes aim at the target. As she stares at it, narrowing her eyes, ready to fire, I flash back on our last year together—nights and days, hopes and dreams, love and dinners and breakfasts and coffees.

She moved in with me at the start of the summer, and the timing fit since Barrett was spending more and more time in the college dorms. He started early at NYU, and he's been living on campus, taking summer classes.

He comes home for dinner a few nights a week, and that's one of my favorite things in the world—seeing him so often, having dinner with him and Peyton as a family. Sometimes Eli joins us, and Rachel too. Eli's going to school in the city, so we'll see if they stay together. For now, Barrett's happy, and that's all I care about.

The edge of the ax wedges itself into the corkboard target, and Peyton thrusts her arms in the air. "Victory is mine."

And I hope she'll be mine forever as she turns around to find me on one knee.

She gasps, her eyes widening. "Oh my God."

I hold open a blue velvet box. "Peyton Marie Valencia, I've loved you for a long time, and I've been the luckiest guy in the world to have you love me back these last months. You're the only woman for me, and I want you to be mine always. I love you. I love you. I love you. Please marry me," I say, echoing the words I shared with her on the street last fall.

I say them without a shred of worry.

Only hope.

Only *love*.

She sinks to the floor, throws her arms around me, and says, "You don't have to ask. I'm already yours forever. I love you, and I'll marry you anytime, any day, anywhere."

A variation on her words that day too.

I slide the ring on her finger, and her eyes light up as she gazes at the diamond solitaire.

"It's gorgeous. I do love shiny objects. But not as much as I love you." She clasps my face and kisses her yes against my lips. Then softly, sweetly, she says, "Thank you for waiting for me."

I kiss her back. "Thank you for asking me to be your research partner."

"You're my permanent research partner now," she says.

"And we'll have a lifetime to experiment."

ANOTHER EPILOGUE

The Lingerie Devotee: Do Try This at a Hotel
Blog entry, My Wedding Night

There's something special about white lace.

It's both innocent and sexual at the same time.

And when I wear it, I feel beautiful too.

That's how I wanted to feel on my wedding night.

No surprise I wore lace, then. White lace bikini panties, white lace garters, and a white lace demi-cup bra. Stockings too. Never forget the stockings.

The lingerie served me well during the ceremony and the reception.

But it served both of us later that night. After all, sometimes the mark of fantastic lingerie is how quickly it comes off.

I believe we set a record.

And we're going to keep setting them for the rest of our lives.

THE END

Eager to know about Lola and the guy who got away? Then be sure to grab ONE NIGHT STAND-IN! It's a sexy, emotional, enemies to lovers, second chance romance.
You'll find this sexy romantic comedy on all retailers! Be sure to sign up for my newsletter to receive an alert when these sexy new books are available! Here is a sneak peek of ONE NIGHT STAND IN!

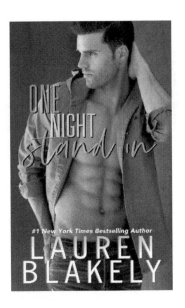

I dart outside and answer the call from my brother. "What's going on?"

"Not much," he says, with a laugh that sounds forced.

"Everything is great."

My hackles go up. "Let me ask again. What's going on now?"

Rowan clears his throat. "Listen, it's no biggie. Everything

is cool. I mean, it will be when we get our stuff back, plus the security deposit, which we're totally going to need. Anyway, I just sent you the email with the details. But there's one little thing I forgot to tell you before we board this cruise."

I groan. "Your stuff isn't in Brooklyn?"

"No. It probably is. I mean, that'd make sense. I'd have to look at the email more closely to know for sure, and I didn't read it yet because it was super long and annoying and messing with my mojo. But that's not the point."

A ship's horn cuts through the phone line, and I can't hear a word he's saying. When the horn ends, he says, "So you don't mind, do you?

"Mind what?" I ask, my jaw ticking, as the May sunshine dares to peek out from behind a cloud. It should be raining. It should be fucking pouring right now.

"You don't mind that Luna asked for help too?"

I let out a sigh of relief. "No, that's fine, of course. It'll be done faster then," I say before I connect the dots. But when I do, all the life leaks out of me. I tense, bracing myself for an answer I don't want. But I have to ask the question. "Who's helping Luna? Is it her sister?"

Please say no, please say no.

I can hear Rowan smile as he answers. "Yes. Lola will help."

Lola Dumont.

Lola fucking Dumont.

I lean against the brick wall of the coffee shop wall, picturing the last time I saw the dark-haired beauty at an industry event. She looked like she wanted to toss her champagne at me. Then deliver a scathing rebuttal of all my mistakes.

Hell, there were things I wanted to say to her too.

When her name pops up in my texts a few minutes later, my brain plays a cruel joke by reminding me of three things.

How much fun we had together for that one year when we were nearly inseparable.

How good her lips tasted that night I kissed her.

And how shitty I felt the weekend after.

Order this sexy romantic comedy now!

ACKNOWLEDGMENTS

Big thanks to Lauren Clarke, Jen McCoy, Helen Williams, Kim Bias, Virginia, Lynn, Karen, Tiffany, Janice, Stephanie and more for their eyes. Much love to Helen for the beautiful cover. Thank you to Kelley and Candi and KP and Jenn. Massive smooches to Laurelin Paige for access to her brain and heart. As always, my readers make everything possible.

ALSO BY LAUREN BLAKELY

FULL PACKAGE, the #1 New York Times Bestselling romantic comedy!

BIG ROCK, the hit New York Times Bestselling standalone romantic comedy!

THE SEXY ONE, a New York Times Bestselling standalone romance!

THE KNOCKED UP PLAN, a multi-week USA Today and Amazon Charts Bestselling standalone romance!

MOST VALUABLE PLAYBOY, a sexy multi-week USA Today Bestselling sports romance! And its companion sports romance, MOST LIKELY TO SCORE!

WANDERLUST, a USA Today Bestselling contemporary romance!

COME AS YOU ARE, a Wall Street Journal and multi-week USA Today Bestselling contemporary romance!

PART-TIME LOVER, a multi-week USA Today Bestselling contemporary romance!

UNBREAK MY HEART, an emotional second chance USA Today Bestselling contemporary romance!

BEST LAID PLANS, a sexy friends-to-lovers USA Today Bestselling romance!

The Heartbreakers! The USA Today and WSJ Bestselling rock star series of standalone!

CONTACT

I love hearing from readers! You can find me on Twitter at LaurenBlakely3, Instagram at LaurenBlakelyBooks, Facebook at LaurenBlakelyBooks, or online at LaurenBlakely.com. You can also email me at laurenblakelybooks@gmail.com